A "The Keys to Love" Novella

A
Folly Beach
Christmas

Miki Bennett

Copyright © 2021 Miki Bennett

Second Edition

ISBN: 978-0-9988481-9-8

WannaDo Concepts Publishing, Charleston, South Carolina

This book is dedicated to all that live courageously
with a chronic illness.

1

As he sat the large box in the now furnished family room, Jason could not help but feel a sense of excitement. This would be his first Christmas in over ten years in a house of his very own. He finally had a place to call home, real roots, and it was all because of Maddy.

Jason had left the job site early to surprise his wife with a very large Christmas tree. Growing up, he had always had live trees, even if they had been brought in by truck to his hometown of Las Vegas, Nevada. He loved the evergreen scent but bringing home a freshly cut tree was not something he was willing to take a chance on with Maddy's health issues. Any new smell, fragrance or chemical could cause her illness to flare, possibly sending her to the emergency room and that was not something Jason was willing to risk. So, an artificial Christmas tree it would be this year but Jason didn't mind. It was their first Christmas together as newlyweds in their recently renovated home on Folly

Beach, near Maddy's hometown of Charleston, South Carolina. Now it was Jason's hometown too. The most important thing was the two of them celebrating the holidays together.

He knew the tree would be easy to put up because that was what he specifically requested. One of those trees that came out of the box and the branches expanded out magically. Jason laughed to himself as he fluffed out the tiny branches because he still couldn't believe he had actually researched Christmas trees on the Internet. He just wanted this to be the best holiday for their new family.

The new picture window in the front of the house would be the magical setting for the brightly lit tree. As he continued to shape branches, he realized he had forgotten ornaments and lights! But then remembered the tree came with its own twinkling illumination. Would that be enough? He would not know till the tree was standing in their home.

Jason wondered if he should have surprised Maddy by putting the tree up or if she would have liked for the both of them to assemble it together but Jason's intuition told him she would be happy either way. It was not long before he plugged the cord into the wall and the tall, expansive Frasier Fir tree seemed to come to life. It would be like a shining star in the window when Maddy got home from the doctor.

Jason hated that he had missed her appointment today but she assured him it was only a check-up. He still had flashbacks to that night he found her almost passed out and in shock on the steps of her Florida Keys rental home. That memory seemed so long ago but he still remembered every detail. Now that they were married and after meeting all her doctors, he realized how serious her predicament truly had been that night. Jason loved this woman more than he thought was possible. He wanted her to be happy but most of all healthy and taking care of her was the one thing he wanted to do for the rest of his life.

Maddy sat in her car only moving inches along Folly Road in the holiday traffic. She usually tried to avoid being in the car this time of day but with a late appointment with her doctor in downtown Charleston at the Medical University Hospital, she had no choice this evening. It was the night before Thanksgiving and everyone was either going out of town for the holiday or shopping for tomorrow's feast. That thought brought a smile to Maddy's face. It was hers and Jason's first Thanksgiving together and they would be having dinner at her parent's home, along with her daughter Hope and her husband Shawn. Her parents had also included their neighbors for the festive occasion. It was going to be a simple affair and she only had to bring the foods she knew she could safely eat. Her mother and Hope were doing the rest of the cooking though Maddy insisted that she could help and actually wanted to be part of the fun in the kitchen.

Maddy thought over this past year and the list of things she had to be thankful for was long. But Jason held the number one spot. She was clearly thankful for her trip to the Florida Keys where she had met and fallen in love with this wonderful man who she was sure was waiting for her at their new home on the island. Jason had shown her that it was okay to love again, to take a chance with someone and she was glad that she had not let him slip through her fingers.

The sun was setting, leaving a faint orange glow on the horizon behind her as she crossed the bridge onto Folly Beach. A few houses already had festive Christmas decorations adorning their exteriors and the yards surrounding them. The sight of the lights excited her. This first holiday season with Jason in their new home at the beach was going to be perfect, she just knew it. He had been so diligent to make sure the work on the house was done on time while simultaneously working on an extremely large project near Beaufort, South Carolina.

When they had met in the Florida Keys, she knew about his career renovating homes and businesses, which he loved, but seeing him in action was something else altogether. He was precise and organized. He was firm but kind with his workers and they loved and respected him. Maddy felt this was why his projects were always done on time or ahead of schedule. This also put Jason in demand for more work than he could handle. And like a business project, Jason applied those same work principles when finishing their home.

She remembered it had only been a short search before they had found a house on Folly Beach that needed a little work. At least that is what Maddy thought but Jason had other plans. He completely renovated it - from the roof to the foundation and everything in between. She had kidded him that they could have built a new house but Jason had insisted from the time of their first inspection that the house had "good bones." Jason had thought of all the details including allergy proofing the house. Windows were placed that would allow the fresh ocean air to circulate throughout the home, when the weather permitted, and they could open up windows and doors. Maddy's doctors had been insistent that the clean air would help with her rare chronic illness.

They had considered moving to the Florida Keys since the little islands had been nearly perfect for Maddy's condition, but she wanted to stay close to family and she already had a team of wonderful doctors treating her in Charleston. Jason did not care where they lived but decided that if it was going to be in South

Carolina, they were going to live on or as close to the beach as possible. And it did not take long to find a house near the ocean.

Their home was only one street from the shoreline - Maddy's happy place. Since they had officially moved in a little over a month ago, she had managed to go to the beach at least every other day, taking nice sandy walks. On the days she felt a little achy due to the cooler weather, she took the golf cart for a ride around the island. Jason had purchased it right after they bought the house. At the time, Maddy thought it was an extravagant purchase, but now, each time she used it, she was secretly grateful.

Pulling into the driveway and looking up at the house, a sudden smile found its way to her face. Beautiful, twinkling lights shown out of the front bay window. A Christmas tree! Her wonderful husband was full of surprises and this one had completely caught her off guard.

"Hey sweetheart," Jason said, making his way down the front steps then pulling Maddy into a loving hug. "Whatcha think?" he said, looking up at the glowing window.

Maddy's gaze followed her husband's. "It's beautiful! I love it but I thought we were going to go looking for trees together? Plus, I usually don't put up the tree till after Thanksgiving. But it looks amazing in the window." Maddy now leaned back, resting against her husband and turned to give him a gentle kiss.

"I can always take it down or take it back," Jason said it with a grin but Maddy shook her head. Neither option was the right one. Her husband had picked out a tree and set it up just for her. To Maddy, it felt like her first real present of the season because he had been thinking of her.

"I think it is perfect and it isn't going anywhere. Now if I could get some more unpacking done, we'll have more room for Christmas decorations."

"We're coming along. It's always a slow process when moving into a new home. Sometimes," Jason said, wrapping Maddy in his arms, "I miss our little apartment."

"Little? It was about the same size as our new house," Maddy laughed as she saw the gleam in Jason's eyes.

"It was definitely smaller. I can give you all the specs."

"I know you can but that's not necessary. Like the elevator that is being installed," Maddy said as she pointed to the construction on the side of the house. "I can climb up and down steps you know."

"Yeah, but I have flashbacks of watching you in the Keys. Climbing those steps was hard on you."

"I need all the exercise I can get and the doctor said steps were good. Just have to be careful, that's all. Make sure I don't overdo it which I'm not."

"Speaking of doctors, how did your appointment go?" Jason asked as they walked toward the house, her tote bag on his arm.

"Same old thing. I'm doing good so keep doing what I'm doing. Told me that marriage seemed to agree with me. When he found out I had made a permanent move to the beach, he was really happy. Says that it'll be the best thing for me but we'll see. I'm not convinced. Plus, it's been colder than normal for Charleston this year, which doesn't usually agree with me, but I'm actually feeling pretty good. Maybe it has something to do with being really happy?" Maddy asked giving her husband another kiss, this time on the cheek, before opening the front door.

When she entered her house, it seemed the bright white lights on the tree filled the entire room with soft, warm glow. She had never had a Christmas tree with lights all of the same color but this was the start of a brand-new chapter in her life. Maddy felt in her heart that she had finally found her soul mate and the thought of that filled her with happiness and brought tears to her eyes. Who would have known her crazy trip to spend a month with her friend, Riley, in the Florida Keys, would have ended up with her meeting the man with whom she knew she was destined to spend the rest of her life.

Maddy got a few things out of her tote bag and saw her phone illuminated, indicating a missed call. She had not heard the ring tone but suddenly remembered that she had turned her phone to "silent" during her doctor's visit. But when she looked at the caller ID, she was shocked to read the name that appeared on the screen: Greg.

Why would he want to talk to her? Maddy had not heard from her ex-husband in over three years. She only knew bits and pieces of Greg's new life when Hope would share tidbits here and there. The last time she had seen or talked to him was that day in court when the judge pronounced their divorce final. Even though she had found a new love and started a new life, the day that Greg had walked out on her still brought back many hurtful memories that haunted her, but the feeling was only slight now that her life was full. But to see his name on her phone after all this time was a bit disconcerting.

"What's wrong?" Jason asked as he watched his wife from the other side of the counter in the kitchen.

"Nothing. Just missed a call – nothing important," Maddy said quickly. "Now, we have to discuss tomorrow. Hope said that all food preparations are done. I have mine ready to go in the frig because no one wants a repeat of my bad judgment last year."

"You never told me anything about Thanksgiving. What happened?" Jason said as he started getting out food for dinner. He tried his best to eat a similar diet to Maddy but her food limitations were at times a bit much too much for him and he would give in to spaghetti sauce, fried chicken and more. Maddy had repeatedly told him many times that it did not matter to her what he ate as long as it was healthy. But Jason had to admit he felt guilty being able to enjoy some delicacies that she could not. At least not right now. He knew she was determined to be able to eat normal meals again eventually.

"I decided to eat my mom's dressing, which I have loved since I was a kid. I hadn't had it in a while and, though it had ingredients I react to, I'd been doing well so I only tried two spoonfuls. Two small spoonfuls! I truly thought it couldn't hurt but it was enough to almost send me to the ER. With Benadryl and a few other meds, I was feeling somewhat normal in about an hour but they came really close to carting me off to the hospital. But those couple of bites was the most wonderful food I'd tasted in quite some time," she said as she put together her plate of mashed potatoes, green beans and a piece of cooked chicken breast and went to sit at the table with Jason.

"I agree. Let's not do that this year." Jason paused, looking across the table at his wife.

"Who was on the phone?"

"When?"

"Your missed phone call a while ago. I know by now when something is bothering you and I saw that look on your face."

Maddy sighed. They may have been together less than a year but it felt like a lifetime to her. The way he could read her was uncanny but she could do the same when it came to him.

"It was Greg."

"Wait - your ex-husband?" Jason asked.

"Yeah. I haven't talked to him since the day our divorce was final and he certainly has never called. Hope mentions him from time to time but that's all. She tries not to talk about him after what happened though I know she loves her Dad. I keep trying to tell her it's okay to talk about him and that it doesn't matter to me."

"After what that idiot did to you, I believe Hope has the right idea. Now that she is married, I think she understands the situation even better," Jason said sternly. "He was wrong and very selfish. A stupid bastard and I hope I never see him."

Maddy watched her husband as he ate his dinner and let the words he spoke sink in. Jason was right. Greg had been cruel over the years as their marriage had dissolved but Maddy had let it go. She had forgiven him. Or had she? Maddy sat there swirling her fork through the food on her plate, thinking.

"I'm sorry. That was a bit harsh" Jason said, looking over to his wife. "But why would he be calling you now?"

"I don't know but I'll ask Hope about it tomorrow. Maybe she knows what's going on. I certainly have no desire to call him back. He's a part of my past. You," she said, reaching over for his hand, "are my present and future." She smiled as Jason took hold of her outstretched hand and gave it a gentle squeeze.

"So, when do we finish decorating the tree and go shopping for presents to put under it?" Jason asked, changing the subject to a much more pleasant one.

"Oh, that's easy. Tomorrow, when we get home from dinner, I'll set the alarm for two o'clock in the morning so we can catch all the Black Friday deals. It's a yearly tradition but I'm usually by myself. As for decorating, let's watch Christmas movies this Sunday and make this house look festive. One problem: we don't have any decorations so that will be on the top of our shopping list." Maddy was excited now, all thoughts of her ex-husband almost completely extinguished.

"You seriously go shopping on the day after Thanksgiving? I tried to go out just to get a hamburger and fries for lunch once and it was like a swirl of cars and people. It's crazy and I can't believe you can even be around all that mess."

"I dress warm, take my breathing mask – you know in case someone decides to bathe in cologne or perfume – pack up some food and shop till I know it's time for me to come home. I've got to keep doing these things. Stay active. It's what helps me to feel normal while dealing with this condition," Maddy said looking at Jason, whose face was showing some concern. "But you make me feel normal too. No, I take that back." She got up and went to him, beckoning him to stand up.

"You make me feel incredible," she said as she placed her hands on each side of his face and reached up to kiss him passionately on the lips. Suddenly she found herself swept up in Jason's arms and she was being carried away from the glow of the Christmas tree toward their bedroom.

2

"I could smell the turkey before we opened the door," Maddy said as they walked into her parent's home. The aroma that wafted to her nose was divine. She stood for a second in the foyer, letting the smells permeate her senses because she was quickly in the holiday spirit. That was until she felt a gentle nudge from behind her.

"Hey sweetheart, I need to get in there," Jason said, carrying the small cooler with Maddy's food plus a few bags of ice that they had been asked to bring.

"I'm sorry," Maddy said, moving quickly out of Jason's way. "You should have let me carry my cooler."

"I got it," Jason said, walking past her and giving her a wink.

Maddy was quickly in the kitchen, where everything felt so inviting and relaxing. For her, this day was the start of the holidays. The special foods. Spending time with family. Talking about all they have to be thankful for this year. Now, she watched as Jason set down her cooler, put the ice in the freezer and give her mother a hug before Maddy had even made it over to where she was standing. Then he headed out to where her father was on the enclosed back porch and they gave each other one of those manly hugs. It was as if Jason had been a part of the family for years, not months. He had fit right into their clan and Maddy felt content as she viewed everything unfolding before her.

Though the scene that played out in front of Maddy brought her joy, she had not been able to forget about the phone call from Greg last evening. Seeing his name on the caller ID of her phone had given her an uneasy feeling, something she could not make sense of and it made her feel uncomfortable. Maddy was counting on Hope to help her. Maybe once she told her daughter about the unexpected phone call, she would be able to shed some light on the subject.

"Hey Momma," Maddy said, finally able to give her mom a hug. "So, what can I do to help?"

"First of all, Happy Thanksgiving" said Maddy's mother, Georgia Newsome, giving her only daughter a hug in return. "Now put the cranberry sauce in the bowl over there. After that the rolls need to go into the oven. Your Dad, bless his heart, couldn't wait so he is already carving the turkey even though I asked him to wait till Hope and Shawn got here. The Jamisons are out back in the sunroom with him. No doubt he and Darren are nibbling on the turkey as it's being cut. I asked Loretta to make sure they didn't eat too much." Maddy looked out the back window and sure enough, everyone was watching her father, Henry, as he stood over the turkey, knife in hand, laughing at something someone had said. Jason was now by his side at the outside table and she saw her husband sneak a bite of the carved meat.

"Are we dining in or out today?" Maddy asked, pointing to the large sunroom. "The weather is perfect for it but I love how festive the dining room looks." Maddy had glanced in the room as she had made her way into the kitchen. Her mother's decorations throughout the house were stunning and Maddy wanted her own home to have the same coziness she felt when she was at the house where she grew up.

"Your Dad was insisting on eating outside but Loretta and I convinced him it would be nice to have all the family around the table inside. Especially with this being Jason's first Thanksgiving with us." Georgia continued their conversation as she finished putting the mashed potatoes into a bowl, going from one task to another.

"Jason doesn't mind whether it is inside or out," Maddy laughed.

"Anyone home?" Maddy heard the voice and smiled. It was her daughter and as Maddy walked around the corner, she first saw her son-in-law then her beautiful baby girl with her swollen tummy. Only a few more months and Maddy would be a grandmother, something she was very excited about. She and Jason had even set aside one of the extra rooms in the new house as a place for what would now be for their new grandchild when he or she would come to visit. Hope's pregnancy was a miracle since she had Type One Diabetes, which put her at a high risk. But everything, so far, was progressing fine, for which Maddy said a prayer of thanks daily.

"You've got your hands full," Maddy said to Shawn, helping him by taking a pumpkin pie he had been precariously carrying on an outstretched arm.

"Thanks! I'm pretty good at balancing things but I definitely don't want to lose any pies. There might be some mighty upset people here if I did," Shawn said and kissed Maddy on the cheek.

"I have marked the ones that are sugar free," Hope said. "I have to have at least a little bit of pie for Thanksgiving. Wouldn't be the same without it."

Mother and daughter, both with life changing medical conditions, but Maddy was glad that neither of them had let it get in their way of living life. Yes, there were times when they both just gave in when not feeling good but Maddy was a fighter and apparently that trait had been passed down to Hope.

"After we have dinner, I want to chat with you for a few minutes," Maddy told her daughter.

"Is everything okay?"

"It's probably nothing but I want to see if you could help me with something."

"No problem," and Hope gave her mom a hug then a kiss on the cheek.

I'm sure she will have the answer, Maddy thought. What kind of answer? What was Maddy expecting? She had thought that part of her life was closed but for some reason, seeing her ex-husband's name last night had kindled a knowing sense of uneasiness she could not erase.

3

"Dishes are officially done!" exclaimed Jason. Maddy cleaned the sink and wiped the counter edges as Jason put the last dish in the above cabinet. The holiday feast had been fabulous, exactly what Maddy had wanted in a Thanksgiving dinner this year.

In her previous marriage, tension always seemed to be in the air around each family gathering. Though her parents had liked Greg until they had found out some of his antics that had affected their daughter, it was nothing compared to how Jason had fit into their lives, as though they had always known him. Even if Maddy and Jason's time together had been short before they got married, Maddy's parents loved Jason, especially when they saw how he treated their daughter through some tough times. It was the trip to Chicago to see one of Maddy's medical specialists that had changed everything. They saw how Jason had been there every step of the way, never backing away from the tough talks, that sealed the deal in their eyes that this was the man for their only daughter.

"Mom, you want to have that talk now?" Maddy turned to see Hope looking a bit drained but sporting a smile. "I think we're going home shortly. I'm feeling kinda tired and need some sleep, I think. And before you ask, I've checked my blood sugar and it's okay," Hope said, knowing exactly what Maddy was thinking.

"Let's sit on the front porch since everyone has congregated in the sunroom. We'll have a bit more privacy," Maddy said as they walked out the door. There was a beautiful oak tree for shade that made the space that lined the front of the house as relaxing as the one gracing the rear of the home.

"So, what's up?" Hope asked, being careful when she sat back in the rocking chair. Maddy took the one beside her daughter and slowly began to rock.

"It's about your Dad. When I got home last night, I saw that I had a missed call from him." Maddy glance over to see if there would be any reaction from Hope, but her daughter sat there looking forward, trying not to close her eyes. "I haven't talked to him in over three years so it surprised me to see his name pop up on my phone. Is there anything going on that I should know about?"

Hope sighed as she continued to look out at the front yard, watching the colorful leaves of the season gently fall from the trees. "Dad's been acting a bit weird lately. At first, I thought it was because I was pregnant. But then I finally got him to talk a little bit and found out that Laney left him, which doesn't surprise me. They never really seemed to 'fit' together, if you know what I mean. But then again, Dad never seems to keep a relationship for long. Well, I should say, since you two divorced."

Maddy sat back in her rocking chair, she too looking out at the peaceful scene in front of her. Thoughts of Greg and what their life had been like when they were together filled her mind. The selfishness. Being alone. Hateful words spoken so harshly. Hardly any help raising their daughter. And then the affair with another woman. In Maddy's mind she had tried to salvage her marriage doing everything she knew to help the situation but to no avail. She had asked herself so many times what she had done wrong. She remembered the times that sadness would seem to swallow her like sinking into the ocean but then anger would spring up to quickly take its place. Then Maddy found out that it was only a little over a month after their divorce was final that Greg remarried. That had hurt more than she thought it would even though Greg's second marriage did not last very long.

Maddy only knew most of this information from the talks she would have with her daughter. Hope would mention something about her father by accident then apologize to her mother. But after the first year of being single again, those emotions did not bother Maddy as much as they had in the beginning. When she met Jason, all those past feelings seemed to have been erased magically or so she thought. She knew with every fiber of her being that Jason had been waiting for her this whole time. That they were meant to be together always. But now there was a twinge inside that had Maddy feeling so out of sorts. It was as though the phone call had triggered emotions Maddy was sure were finally healed. Why would she be concerned about a phone call from her ex-husband now that she felt whole again? But the nagging feeling would not go away.

"Well, I have no idea why he'd call me. We have no connections at all except you. I was even surprised he still had my number."

"I know when we had lunch not too long ago, he mentioned you. Wanted to know how you were doing. And about your wedding to Jason."

"What did you say?"

"I told him the truth. You were doing good. That your wedding was wonderful and that Jason was the best thing to happen to you. I'm sorry Mom, but the words slipped out before I thought. I didn't want to hurt Dad but it's true. I've never seen two people more in love than when I watch you and Jason together. I know it was never like that between you and Dad. He was always so distant. Even the times when I was really sick, he never seemed to be there," Hope said, her voice fading softly.

"But I still love him. I can't help it – he's my Dad. I will say that I can see some change in him like he's a bit softer around the edges," she said with a slight laugh. "I know what he did was bad and it has taken a long time for me to come to terms with it but he does seem different except for when it comes to romantic relationships. Goodness he has a lot to learn."

Maddy smiled slightly and could not help but notice how astute her daughter was. She was right. Greg had shirked his duty as a father even before he left her. He had never been the man or father that Maddy had thought he would be when they found out, unexpectedly, that Maddy was pregnant. She kept hoping Greg would take being a father seriously, but he never did. And Hope's medical problems only made him more distant.

Talking with Hope was causing Maddy some mild anxiety as she relived so many memories that she thought had been put on a shelf in her mind. When Greg told her he was leaving, it had only been one week after Hope's wedding. Maddy could remember his exact words: "I don't want to do this anymore." He then proceeded quickly to pack up two suitcases and said he would be back later for the rest of his things. Maddy also remembered feeling so defeated because she had felt this was coming but did not know when.

Greg never showed up for his belonging and one day Maddy, in a fit of anger, put all his stuff in boxes and dumped everything she could on the lawn in front of his new home. Hope had helped her, so mad at her father at the time. But that was when Maddy found out that Greg had been seeing someone new before their divorce was final. A young woman walked out to confront Maddy about dumping trash on her lawn and after a very short conversation all the details of Greg's other life were revealed. He had not had just one affair but many. And now within a few weeks of leaving Maddy, his wife of twenty-five years, he was already in someone else's arms and soon after, married.

The divorce had taken longer than both Greg and Maddy wanted. Greg admitted to the affairs in hopes of taking care of the divorce quickly but it took time. As soon as he had his freedom, though, it was not long before there was another ring on his finger. The hurt Maddy felt was hard. She had known her marriage was not rock solid but when they were together, she kept hoping that they would be able to fix what was wrong, especially once Hope was out on her own. She had even thought they could move past his relationships with other women. But Maddy suddenly remembered the day that Greg told her that the only reason he had waited to get out of the marriage was because he wanted to walk Hope down the aisle at her wedding. He knew if he left sooner, Hope would not have allowed it. *So selfish*, Maddy thought to herself as she replayed old memories.

"Mom, I will say he has been saying weird stuff. I personally think he might even be depressed. I've tried talking to him but it's still hard. I don't want things to go back to how they were when Dad first left because we finally have some semblance of a relationship. But he keeps saying things like 'I'm no good', 'I should've never left' and 'What am I going to do now'. I keep asking him what's going on and his only answer is 'nothing'."

Maddy could feel anger rising up inside of her and with her next words, her voice was louder than she intended. "He certainly doesn't need to be bothering you right now. Stress is the last thing you need! He was horrible to you, to me, to everyone. Selfish, mean, uncaring. And it didn't bother him. Even when you refused to talk to him that first year, I never wanted you to be estranged from him since he was your dad but you had every right." Maddy could feel her heart beating faster and she was getting flushed. She could feel the tension growing by the minute. All the pain that she was positive had disappeared was suddenly back.

"I'm sorry. I didn't mean to say anything to upset you but you asked. As to why he would be calling – I honestly don't know. Don't answer the phone. If he says anything to me, I'll tell him you have a new life and that he needs to leave you alone," Hope said.

"I shouldn't have brought you into this, especially right now," Maddy said, reaching over to pat Hope's baby bump. "And I'm sorry I got so upset. Old memories. Just seeing his name on the phone left me feeling out of sorts."

"Why is his number and name still in your phone?" her daughter asked.

"I only kept it in case I needed to talk to him if there was something concerning you."

"Okay, that makes sense."

Maddy took a deep breath and stood up. "Listen, you go on home. You and my grandbaby need to get some rest. Do I still have to wait to find out the sex of my grandchild?"

Hope laughed. "You'll find out Christmas Day, like everyone else."

"But I'm your mom. Doesn't that give me some brownie points? I promise if you tell me I won't say a word to anyone else," Maddy whined, trying to concentrate on something happier than the thoughts and memories she was having only moments ago.

"It's been very hard not to tell anyone but now that it's getting close and I'm past that critical stage, just think how special Christmas Day will be."

"You are a stubborn child," Maddy said with a smile to her daughter.

"Like my momma!"

Mother and daughter walked back into the house, Maddy's arm wrapped around Hope's shoulder. "Well, I think it's cruel. I'm sure Shawn's parents are as curious as we are."

Hope looked at her mom and took her hands. "You're going to make a wonderful grandma, you know that?"

"I plan to spoil her rotten!" Maddy said, looking for a reaction on Hope's face.

"Sorry, that won't work," Hope said, laughing at her mom.

"Ugh, then Christmas Day it is."

4

"Were you able to find out anything from Hope?" Jason asked as they pulled out of the driveway to head home after dinner.

"Only that Greg's girlfriend left him and, using Hope's words, her Dad has been acting weird. That's all she knew or at least that was all she would share. I have to admit I got a little upset as we were talking because memories of everything that happened during our marriage and when he left seemed to surface again. And I don't understand." Maddy looked over to her husband. "I have you now. Those things shouldn't faze me. I hadn't even thought about them in such a long time. But seeing his name yesterday and talking about him today brought back a lot of hurt that I thought was long gone."

"Just because your life has changed and for the better, if I do say so myself," Jason said, grinning at her, "doesn't mean your past magically goes away. Shoot, mine came back to haunt me big time when we were in the Keys. I'm glad you were there to help me."

Maddy smiled as she remembered Jason's ex-wife, Andrea, coming to the Florida Keys to extort money from him but her plan had backfired. Now she and her accomplice were in prison.

"Don't you remember how angry I was when Andrea showed up?" Jason asked.

"Yes, but this is different."

"How?"

"Because I was positive that all those feelings were gone or at least faded away. You know, like it was sealed up and put away someplace that it couldn't hurt me anymore. I had forgiven him for everything that had happened or at least I thought so. Talking to Hope brought it all back, almost like it happened only months ago. The feeling was so odd."

"Maddy – it hasn't been that long ago. In the grand scheme of things, it's only been a little over three years. You need to give yourself a break."

"But what does that mean about me and you?" Maddy asked, her voice shaking.

"What do you mean?"

"I love you Jason. More than any man I have ever known and I truly, undeniably feel that we are meant to be together. As cliché as this sounds, you're my soul mate – I know that more than anything. So why am I still letting my ex dictate my feelings? Does that mean something is wrong with me?" Tears began to form in the corners of her eyes and Maddy tried to keep them from gliding down her cheeks.

Jason reached over and took her hand in his. "There is definitely nothing wrong with you. I love you with every fiber of my being and I know you love me too. You were dealt a tough hand and sometimes those things take time to heal. A lot of time. I think that's part of the reason we met. You've helped me deal with some of my past that I thought had no control over me and now I'm here to help you. It doesn't mean that our marriage isn't strong. Personally, I think we have the best relationship around. Hell, I think we should write a book of advice to all newlyweds on every 'do and don't' before and after the ceremony," Jason said giving her the sexy grin that had first intoxicated her in the Florida Keys.

Jason's assessment of the situation lessened the tension in the car. Maddy laughed a little at his remark. "I do believe you're right. Between the two of us, we certainly have quite a few experiences that we could share," Maddy said, gently brushing the tears off her cheeks, "and the lessons we learned."

Now her wish was that between Hope talking to her father and Maddy not returning his call that Greg would leave her alone. But she also knew she had some personal soul searching to do. Today had revealed there were parts of her past that still needed to heal.

"Do we really have to do this?" Jason said, yawning as he pulled his shirt over his head. He looked at the clock once more to see that they were indeed up at two o'clock in the morning.

Maddy had come home from Thanksgiving dinner and promptly took a shower, ate a snack, and laid out her clothes for their morning shopping excursion. After crawling into bed and before falling asleep, she went through the stack of newspaper inserts for the big sales that took place on Black Friday, putting a plan in place for each store she wanted to visit.

"I do this every year. I have to say the last ten or so have been a bit more challenging, even before I knew about my illness but I still made a way. That's why I get everything ready the night before, set the alarm clock, and then head off. Be thankful that I didn't want to start last night and go all night plus some today," Maddy said, giving him a teasing look.

Jason rolled his eyes but smiled. He knew she was only kidding because he could tell she was tired. But he also knew that she could go on adrenaline if there was something she wanted to do. Jason loved seeing her this excited but he also did not want her to do too much and jeopardize her health.

He knew he walked a fine line where Maddy was concerned. Jason's instincts were to do everything for her: protecting her, making sure that she wanted for nothing and she did not have to lift a finger. But he was also aware that doing those things would not be the right thing for her either. Maddy had to keep active, go places, try new things and more, being careful along the way.

Jason knew how to help her when things did not always go as planned like quickly giving her medication only a few weeks ago after they went for a walk on the pier at the beach and the sun proved too much for her. It was times like that Jason wanted to shield her from the world, but Maddy was tough. So, he let her call the shots, staying in the background as much as possible and gently reminding her at times when she needed to slow down. Shopping in the wee hours of the morning seemed a little overboard but he would go along with it. Plus, he had to admit that doing something different like this for the holidays and with Maddy made this shopping trip sound like fun.

"Are you ready?" Maddy said, bounding into the kitchen like a child. "I have our whole route planned out along with a shopping list for each store. And the first place I want to go to is the craft supply shop. I need to stock up on watercolor paper and paint. Plus, I want to try some new markers and buy some supplies to make jewelry. I used to do that so long ago and I loved it but didn't have much time. Just think? What if my designs were to end up in a magazine or something?"

"Well, if anyone can do it, it would be you sweetheart but that list looks a bit long," Jason said gesturing at the paper in her hand. "We'll be gone all day."

"Oh no. I have it all mapped out so don't worry. My first Black Friday shopping day with you! I'm so excited!" She gave him a quick kiss on the lips before getting a snack out of the refrigerator along with the food she had for them for the day.

"Yeah, so am I," Jason said with mocked enthusiasm.

"I promise you're going to have fun. Plus, there is one store in particular I know you're going to thoroughly enjoy," Maddy said with a wink. "And we need to get some Christmas decorations for the tree and the house. Hey, you do want to decorate the outside of the house, right?"

"Why don't we get on the road and we can discuss it." Those must have been magic words. Jason almost laughed as he watched his wife grab everything she needed and move fast to the front door.

Once they were on their way, Jason was surprised there were more cars than normal for so early in the morning but no traffic jams that he was sure would occur later in the day. As they drove to their first stop, they made the decision to decorate the outside of their new home but Jason would not have the time. They would hire someone that could help. Maddy was sure that Shawn might have a friend that could probably do the work and love the extra cash, especially this time of year. So, they added the necessary outdoor decorations they would need to Maddy's growing shopping list.

"You know, since this is your first Christmas in Charleston, there is so much I want to show you. I looked on the Internet and found that almost every night there is an event or place we can go for Christmas festivities. Almost an endless list of things we can do. What does your work schedule look like?" Maddy asked, already turning the page in her notebook to write down their holiday schedule.

"We're taking a two-week Christmas break on the Beaufort project. The guys have been working hard and we're ahead of schedule. So, I'll be all yours from the seventieth of December through the second of January. Think you can stand for your husband to be around twenty-four hours a day for a couple of weeks?" Jason asked, grinning over at Maddy as he touched her cheek.

"I wish it was that way all the time," Maddy replied, reaching up to put her hand over his. "Now that I know, I can plan our Christmas activities. There's so much we can do."

"I know you want to show me everything but I'm fine with a quiet Christmas at home. I don't want you to over extend yourself. We're going to be spending lots of Christmases together so we don't have to do everything at once."

"You need to quit worrying so much about me," Maddy said.

"I can't help it."

"And I love that but I'm so excited this year. These are the things that Gr..." She almost said his name but stopped herself. Maddy suddenly remembered all the things Greg would do, very begrudgingly, or not at all. Events that she would sometimes be by herself because he would decide at the last minute he did not want to go. Now, she had someone who really wanted to share the holidays with her. Like going shopping during the early morning hours the day after Thanksgiving. It was a time she looked forward to each year even if she did not buy much of anything. Greg would only stand there and act annoyed, if he even went with her at all.

"You know you can say his name," Jason said softly. "Our relationship is rock solid though when I do hear it, I get a bit ticked off thinking about what he did to you. But let's just try to move past it. If Hope talks to him, like she said she would, his number shouldn't be showing up on your phone anymore."

Maddy shook her head, looking straight ahead to the dark road in front of them. She could feel some of those deep emotions creeping up to the surface again, from being so excited about this early morning shopping trip with Jason to the thought of her ex-husband's name bringing her crashing down with thoughts about her past. But she was not going to let this ruin her very first Christmas with the new man in her life.

"Okay, so back to my list. There's the boat parade that takes place around the Charleston Harbor, which is fun but can be a little bit cold. Of course, shopping downtown on King Street and at the Market. Love the way everything is decorated there. We have to go to James Island County Park for the Festival of Lights. It was voted one of the top Christmas light shows in the country. Oh, and watching Christmas movies under the stars outside at the park. We always bring snacks, drinks," Maddy said before Jason interrupted.

"Wow, I thought you meant only a few things. I don't think I've ever done that many holiday activities during the season, even when I was a young boy."

"There's so much to do and I want to do it all. This year is so different, sharing it with you," Maddy said. "I wish your parents could be here, too."

"Well, I couldn't tell them to turn down a free trip to Hawaii even though I think they would've. My mom is tickled pink that I'm finally married to a nice girl," Jason said with a laugh. "Every time I talk to her, she gushes that her baby is married and how much she loves you."

They pulled into the parking lot of the craft store, a line of people already formed at the door. Maddy sighed looking at the people.

"What's wrong?" Jason asked.

"They'll be opening in a few minutes. Though I should probably get in line to make sure I get that paper I want, I think I'll stay in the car where it's warm. The other supplies I'm looking for probably aren't as in demand as some of their other sale items," Maddy said as Jason pulled into the parking space that was as close to the store entrance as possible with all the holiday shoppers already there. He could tell Maddy was tired this morning but she had not said a word. She was too excited about shopping and for the first time, Jason could not believe he was too. Not to shop but to see the look of enjoyment on his wife's face and spend time with her. He just smiled as he gazed at her.

"What?" Maddy asked, looking over to see Jason staring at her.

"I love you," Jason said so sweetly that it sent tingles all the way to Maddy's toes.

"And I love you too," she replied. She was still basking in the glow of what everyone was telling her was the "honeymoon" stage of hers and Jason's relationship. She did not care what stage it was. She only knew that she wanted to soak up every minute of it, hoping this feeling would never go away.

"They're opening the doors! Here we go," and she opened the car door quickly.

"Wait for me," Jason cried out to her.

"You're going in with me?" Maddy asked.

"Unless you don't want me to."

"No, I'd love for you too. I'm so used to doing this by myself."

Jason put his arm around her shoulders, pulling her closely to him as they walked toward the building. "Well guess what? Now you don't have to."

They entered the store, people everywhere and Jason was amazed at Maddy's quickness for such an early morning. She secured a shopping cart and headed straight to the department that carried the art supplies she needed. Jason followed behind, watching her walk. He could gaze at this woman every second and never get enough. Sharing their first holiday season together and making their own traditions was going to be so special. Except next time, he noted, he would remember to bring his own thermos of coffee.

He continued to watch Maddy in action as she turned down the aisle toward her paints and watercolor paper. She was an excellent artist and he had convinced her to put her artwork online. She was selling prints now and doing rather well. They had hired a web designer, giving her a glowing site that attracted many visitors. But he had also hired someone to do the office work for her because Maddy's heart was in her painting and some photography. What really helped her, and Jason knew it, was the fact that she was contributing to their family. She was using her creativity to help, which built her confidence, plus helped her deal with the stress of her medical issues.

"Did you find what you needed?" Jason asked as he finally caught up with her.

"Yep! Paint refills, larger paper and a few new brushes. Now, to the jewelry supplies. I think I might be able to sell some jewelry too and the holidays are the best time to try it," Maddy said as they started to head to the other side of the store. But as she turned the corner, she suddenly stopped, unable to move.

"Greg!"

Maddy's breath caught in her throat and her heart started beating hard in her chest. Her ex-husband was standing at the end of her cart. He had not changed much since the last time she had seen him. He looked a little bit heavier and his hair was almost all silver gray. Even with the slight changes, she had immediately recognized him.

"Hi Maddy," Greg said calmly.

"What are you doing here?" Maddy asked, still in a state of disbelief.

"Shopping, like you. Getting some more supplies. I started using my acrylic paints again and have a few commission paintings I need to finish before Christmas. I remembered how good the discounts were today." Maddy had not taken her eyes off of him, still stunned to see Greg in the store.

"Hi. I'm Jason Burnett, Maddy's husband," Jason said firmly, stepping in front of his very still wife and reaching his hand toward Greg.

"Nice to meet you," Greg said in a pleasant but monotone voice, shaking Jason's hand. "I've heard good things about you from Hope."

"Thanks," Jason replied. He wanted to say more but knew at the moment the words would not have been friendly so he held his tongue. But he stood beside Maddy and put his arm around her waist. Jason immediately could feel that Maddy seemed to be shaking from head to toe.

"Well, we have some other things to get and more shopping that needs to be done," Jason said as pleasantly as he could. "Ready, sweetheart?" he asked and that brought Maddy's attention to him.

As Maddy looked at Jason, she felt like she had zapped back to reality. Why had the appearance of Greg shocked her so much?

"Yes, we need to go. Good luck with your paintings," and Maddy pushed the cart past Greg, Jason following her.

"Maddy?"

She stopped slowly, squeezed her eyes closed tight before opening them again then turned around to her ex. "Yes?"

"I tried to call you the other day but didn't get an answer. Was wondering if you had a few minutes so we could talk."

"What do you want?" Her voice was shaking but with Jason's hand on her waist, she felt a bit stronger.

"Just something I want to talk to you about."

"You can tell me here."

"No offense but was hoping it could be a private conversation between the two of us," Greg said, no expression coming through his voice.

"It doesn't matter. Whatever we talk about, I'll be sharing with my husband," Maddy said with much emphasis because now she felt a little anger rising up inside of her.

"If you would, give me a call back. Hopefully you still have my number on your phone. Merry Christmas," Greg said, walking away from them, toward the painting supplies.

Maddy turned and started walking fast, not saying a word.

"Hey, slow down," Jason said "Are you okay?"

"Why is he here? Today of all days! This is my special day, to start the holidays. He knows that." Then it hit her: she did not take his call the other day and he knew of her yearly tradition.

"He knew."

"Knew what?" Jason asked, perplexed.

"That I would be here. This is always the first store I come to so I can get art supplies. When we were together, he usually would sit in the car unless he needed paint. He knew. But why does he want to talk to me? There is nothing to discuss and I certainly don't want to talk to him!" Maddy said in an irritated whisper as they stood in the checkout line.

"Then don't. Personally, I wanted to tell him to go to hell but I figured I'd let you handle the situation unless you needed my help. But you don't need this added stress. If he bugs you anymore, just tell him you don't want to talk and to leave you alone. Block his number on your phone if you have to. If he doesn't get the message, I'll take care of it."

"I'm fine. I can handle it - just a bit irritated at the moment." She looked around and saw him way in the back of the line that was beginning to loop around the store aisles. "Let's just get out of here. I can get these things later."

"Hey, we're next to check out," Jason said softly, trying to help Maddy calm down. "Listen. It's okay. Let's think of something else. Where are we going next?"

Maddy stood there, gazing in front of her. She could not think straight and that frustrated her. This man, this person whom she thought she was done with, was back in her life. And all she could think of was why. Why did he want to talk? Did she want to hear what he had to say? *Are you kidding*, Maddy said to herself?

"No way!" she said out loud.

"What was that?" Jason looked at her with a confused look.

"I'm sorry. Thinking to myself and got a bit carried away."

Within a few minutes, they were walking out of the store, bags in hand, but she looked back one last time to see Greg looking at her with a smile. It almost made her nauseous.

"Now that 'that' is behind us, where to next? I know you had a big list and I'm ready to shop. At least till my stomach starts growling which could be anytime." Jason was doing his best to distract her and little by little it started working. As they headed to the next store, Maddy began talking about the items she wanted to look for, the Christmas decorations they would need and before Jason knew it, the Maddy that he knew was back to the bubbly woman that started out on the shopping journey this morning.

Even though Jason did not say anything or act differently, he was seething inside. Something was going on and he wanted to know what it was. There was no coincidence that Maddy's ex-husband should call then they run into him only a few days later. If he had to, he would talk to Greg and tell him to leave her alone. But only if he started to see it was affecting Maddy more than it already was. He had someone precious to take care of and she meant everything to him because Maddy was his now.

5

"I swear you bought out each store we went to," Jason said as he sat down the last of the bags from their morning of shopping. Maddy had slumped into a chair in the family room with a very contented smile on her face.

"That was so much fun," she said, her voice very tired.

"It was and I know you want to probably put things up, decorate – whatever, but would you please listen to your wonderful, loving husband and take a break? I can see you are very tired," Jason said, scooting in to sit beside her in the oversized chair and wrapping her into his arms.

"It has been a long day but so much fun. We got presents, baby stuff, and decorations. But you're right," Maddy said. "I'm going to take a shower, put my pajamas on then fix some lunch. Maybe watch a Christmas movie. I wanted to walk to the beach but I'll save that for tomorrow. I think we definitely got our exercise this morning. Maybe we could go watch the sunrise tomorrow morning then take that beach walk," she said looking up at her husband.

"Two early days in a row? Not for this guy on a holiday weekend," Jason said, kissing the tip of Maddy's nose. "But a beach walk always sounds good. As for now, I'll fix some food and put a fire in the fireplace while you put on your PJs."

"Watch a Christmas movie with me?"

"What if I sit with you. I need to go over some e-mails."

"That sounds good. I'm off to take a shower." Maddy carefully got up, extricating herself from Jason's arms as he had closed his eyes. She smiled as she looked at him knowing that probably before she even made it to the shower, he would be lightly snoring in the chair.

The warm water ran over her body, releasing the tension of the day. Maddy had done her best not to show any repercussions from running into Greg so Jason would not worry, but seeing him had disturbed her more than she thought it would. It felt so strange: her ex-husband in front of her and Jason standing beside her. Maddy had an innate feeling that there was something going on. More than Hope had said. Greg had not spoken to her in so long so she wondered at the possibilities. Was he sick? Was he moving? Going away? *That would be great,* Maddy thought quickly except for the fact that he would not see his grandchild. *Damn!! We'll be seeing more of each other when the baby is born!*

Maddy thought suddenly but she was sure Hope would take care of that situation. Maddy could not seem to shut off the continuous flow of thoughts about her ex-husband.

"Stop!" Maddy said aloud then hoped the shower water had muted her voice. There was so much to do and show Jason during this special time of the year and she was determined that this holiday season would help her release these hurtful feelings about her past.

It seemed like the Christmas activities in Charleston were endless. Thinking about the short list she had already told Jason about, Maddy decided that as soon as she was settled in front of the TV with her laptop, she would hunt down more possible things they could do. It was exciting to have someone in her life for the first time that she could truly share the holidays with – every event, movie, church service, and more. Maddy's ex-husband had never seemed to enjoy the season except when they were buying toys for Hope. If there had been other times, Maddy could not recall them nor did she want to anymore. Now she had Jason.

She made her way into the kitchen in her pajamas including the fuzzy socks she loved so much. Jason had indeed started a fire in the fireplace, heating up the family room nicely. And then she looked over to see him now stretched out on the couch, sleeping like a baby. She placed some food in the microwave to heat up for lunch. She did not want to disturb Jason's nap but the sounding buzzer on the appliance woke him like an alarm clock sounding off.

"Hey, why don't you go to the bedroom and get some sleep? I think I got you out of bed a bit early this morning," Maddy said, laughing softy as she came into the room with her plate of food. "I'm going to put on the movie and do some research on the computer."

Jason stretched, looked over at his wife who did indeed look like she was ready for bed at one o'clock in the afternoon. "Thought I was going to watch a movie with you."

"I think you need some more sleep, even before you check those emails. You aren't used to the Black Friday shopping tradition so you need some more rest," she teased him. "I've been in training for years."

"What are you researching on the computer?"

"I'm making sure I've checked out all the activities for our Christmas vacation. Well, let's call it a 'staycation'. Remember the things I told you about earlier? I want to put everything on a calendar. This way I can completely envelope you in the sounds and sights of Christmas in Charleston."

Jason smiled and shook his head. "Don't over plan because then we will both be stressed. I want a nice, relaxing Christmas with my wife," he said as he reached her side and kissed her so intensely, she almost dropped her plate of food. "And even though I can handle early morning shopping marathons, I'll take you up on that nap suggestion. Do you need anything?"

"I'm all set except for one more thing."

"What?"

"Thanks for this morning. I had so much fun sharing it with you." This time Maddy gave him a passionate kiss before telling him "I love you."

"I love you too," Jason said as he winked at her and turned to walk to the bedroom.

She settled into the chair, her food on one side and her water on the other. She propped her feet up on the ottoman where she kept her fluffy blanket. She took the laptop out of its protective sleeve in her tote bag and set it beside her. But before Maddy turned the TV on to find a Christmas movie, she looked around the room. The tree, the shopping bags and the fireplace felt so homey and it made her smile, inside and out.

"I can't wait for you to see this," Maddy said, as they turned onto Riverland Drive.

"No offense but from the pictures I saw, it is just a bunch of Christmas lights," Jason said, wanting to show enthusiasm for the light display Maddy had told him so much about. Though the day had been long at work, he had promised Maddy they would go to see the lights tonight. Jason would have been content to stay home and watch TV, cuddling with his wife on their very comfortable sofa as they sat by the decorated Christmas tree in their home.

Much to Jason's surprise, after their shopping spree on Friday, Maddy had indeed marked their calendar almost every day with some sort of holiday activity. Jason wondered if they would ever be home but he did not have the heart to tell his wife that the only thing he wanted during the holiday season was to be with her. It truly felt like his first Christmas to be with someone special.

"Okay, turn here," Maddy said as a huge lighted sign came into view. They were finally at the James Island County Park where the "Festival of Lights", an annual holiday event, was a Charleston tradition. Maddy had given him all the details from how the event began so small and had grown to one of the largest holiday light shows in the United States. Jason was pretty impressed by the few displays he saw as they entered the park.

"Wow, these are pretty bright and big. Plus, I can't believe the long line of cars," he said as they inched along to pay the entrance fee.

"You're going to love it. They also have a place where you can stop and walk around. I think they call it Santa's Village or Winter Wonderland. You can roast marshmallows, shop for Christmas goodies and they have food to eat. Plus, you get to walk through the woods that are decorated with lights. I've never been before but Hope has told me all about it."

"Why haven't you stopped there before?" Jason asked as they continued moving in line.

"No one ever wanted to go," Maddy said, sounding slightly melancholy.

"You mean your ex never wanted to go."

"Well, yes. I could barely get him to come to the light show at all. Hope usually talked him into it."

"Well then, if you are up to it, we are roasting marshmallows tonight!" Jason said.

"Really?" Maddy asked excitedly. "You don't mind?"

Jason moved the car up slightly then looked over at her. "Maddy, I'm not him. I know it's hard not to compare because of what happened in the past. But it's you and me now. What you described sounds like a lot of fun. But can you have marshmallows?"

"I haven't tried one in years so I really don't know. Maybe a small bite?"

"I don't want to have to take you to the doctor."

"I'll be careful – promise," she said smiling from ear to ear with excitement.

The light show proved to be every bit the festive spectacle that Maddy had described, Jason thought. She told him the county park had over seven hundred displays featuring colorful Christmas lights and he had to drive slow enough to see the lights that glowed on either side of the road. At one point they even drove under a colorful canopy of what seemed like twinkling stars.

Maddy had pictures of the festival from years past but that did not stop her from taking one picture after another because this was a new beginning in her life. These photos were for her and Jason.

"I think this is the turn off for Santa's Village. Feeling up to it?" Jason asked.

"Oh yes! And I've got everything with me to bundle up since its cold outside."

"Just promise me that if you start to feel bad at any time, we'll leave. None of this 'I'll suck it up' stuff, okay?"

"Promise," Maddy said, holding up her right hand as if she was swearing an oath.

They parked the car then slowly made their way through the wooded area of lighted trees and dancing lights. They saw sand sculptures and a Christmas train taking children and adults on an adventure through the lights. A display of giant greeting cards were also greeted them on their walk. They had been made by local students that showed a wealth of talent along with a lot of holiday cheer. But what caught Maddy's eye were the giant fire pits and the people roasting the rather large marshmallows on huge, long sticks.

"This looks like fun!" she said, quickly walking toward the fire. But she suddenly stopped, as a sharp pain seemed to penetrate her chest.

"What's wrong?" Jason asked as he practically ran into the back of her.

"Just a little hard to take a breath. Must be the cold."

"Then we need to leave."

"Not before we roast marshmallows, please?"

"You know the cold can trigger a reaction and even though you are bundled up, maybe it's too much. I don't want to see you end up in the ER."

"It's getting better. I'll just slow down. If it happens again, we'll leave. I promise," Maddy said, disappointment welling up inside of her. She wanted to do this so badly but she knew that the weather sometimes did not agree with her body. She was layered with clothing, scarves, gloves and hats, and still her body wanted to rebel. *Just get through this*, she told herself and willed her body to listen. As she stood still, her breathing started to return to normal and the pain was subsiding.

"I'll go stand by the fire and get warm while you get the marshmallows," Maddy said, looking up at her husband, seeing his worried face. "I promise, I'm okay."

Jason took a deep breath and sighed. "That's probably a good idea. But you promise you're feeling better?"

"Promise."

As Jason walked away, Maddy looked around, soaking in the atmosphere. Hope was right – this was fun, almost magical. Everyone seemed so happy. Watching the children made her think of her own grandchild who would be here soon and maybe this time next year, they could bring her here. At least Maddy was counting on a little girl even though now it really didn't matter to her if it was a boy or a girl, as long as mother and child were safe and healthy.

"Here you go ma'am," Jason said as he handed her a stick with three giant marshmallows. She put them over the big fire, just high enough not to get burned but to turn a nice dark, toasty brown. Then she took a big bite of the marshmallow with all its gooeyness. Maddy took one more bite, wanting to eat the whole thing but knew that was all she could try this time. She would have to see if this food would agree with her or not. But if there were no consequences, she would make sure that she and Jason definitely came back for more before the beautiful display was taken down.

"Taste good?"

"The best! I haven't had this in so long. Takes me back to my childhood when we used to roast marshmallows all the time. You want the rest of mine?"

"Of course! Can't let a good roasted marshmallow go to waste."

"Wait! Do you have your phone?"

"Yeah but what's wrong?"

"Nothing. I just want a selfie pic with the marshmallows and I left my phone back in the car."

Jason took the picture then finished both his and her treats before they took a slow walk back to the car. He put his arm around her, trying to keep her warm by having her close to him but he also loved wrapping himself around her. He never knew a relationship could feel like this and he thanked God every day for the love of this woman.

"Wow, its colder than I thought," Maddy said as they sat in the car waiting for it to warm up. She reached in her purse for the extra set of gloves she had brought only to see her phone screen lit with a notification. A missed call from Greg once again. She stared at the phone then leaned her head back on the seat.

"What's wrong?" Jason asked as he backed the car out of its place and headed out to finish the tour around the park.

"I have another missed call from Greg."

"Seriously? You didn't block his number?"

"I forgot. He even left a message this time."

"What does it say?" Jason asked, trying to do his best to keep his temper in check.

Maddy pressed the "play" button and they both proceeded to listen as Greg once again expressed his desire to speak to Maddy and for her to please call him.

"Maddy, not that I want you to talk to him or press you in that direction but don't you kinda want to know why he is so insistent on talking to you? Personally, I'd like to tell him to leave you alone because he's pissing me off but I'm trying to keep my mouth shut."

She sat there for a few moments, staring out the window at the lights as they continued to go past colorful Christmas displays and under a few lights that gave the illusion like dripping ice. It seemed like every time she finally thought she had a handle on her past life with Greg, he seemed to pop back into her life. Maddy remembered the conversation in the store. She thought she had been adamant in the fact that she wanted nothing to do with Greg but it was very apparent that he was not listening.

"I'm slightly curious but I don't want to talk to him. I get so angry just thinking about his phone calls. I can't even imagine sitting face to face and trying to have a civil conversation."

"You have every reason to feel that way. I did the same thing with Andrea but you helped me through it. Now I just feel sorry for her and don't think about her much at all. Maybe if you talked to him, you could get this pent-up frustration out of your system and help you heal that part of your past. And let him know how you feel in the process."

"But I don't feel anything for him!" Maddy exclaimed.

"Of course you do! Look how angry you are right now."

Jason was right. Here she was surrounding by Christmas lights on every side but feeling frustration about a man that she did not want in her life again. Maddy would have to think about it because the thought of having a sit-down talk with her ex-husband that had nearly destroyed her life and her self-esteem made her stomach lurch. She would have to do something though to stop this madness because she was not going to let this ruin her first Christmas with Jason.

6

"I can't believe it's only two weeks till Christmas," Maddy said as she and Hope sat, curled up on the couch watching a Christmas movie.

"And I have finished my shopping. That's even a bigger surprise," Hope said as she gently rubbed her growing abdomen but with a frown on her face. "Thank goodness for online shopping. No standing in lines, waiting for people or dealing with crazy drivers in crowded parking lots."

"You sound a bit frustrated or upset. What's going on?" Maddy asked her daughter.

"I don't know. Just, every year I've been able to go out and do things. This year, I'm stuck going nowhere. Well, at least I can come to your house. Don't get me wrong because I'm excited about the baby but I wish the doctor would lighten up my restrictions. Or at least not tell Shawn. I think he is worse than you ever were while I was growing up," Hope said as she tried to relax with her feet propped up.

"Be very thankful you have a man that's really looking out for you and loves you very much. You might not be able to do some things but you can go look at Christmas lights by either riding through the county park, or going over to Park Circle. There are tons of Christmas movies on and all you have to do is ask any of your friends to come over for a quick party and they'd be there in a flash."

Maddy knew all too well how Hope was feeling because she went through the same thing from time to time. The days where she was either too sick or extremely fatigued that the thought of leaving the house was monumental. Sometimes Maddy would push through the feelings only to deal with the consequences later but sometimes she just had to be outside or doing something other than lying around. It was a very fine line she walked.

"Besides, think about next Christmas. That little baby boy is going to make it really special!" Maddy said, waiting once again to see a reaction on her daughter's face.

Hope started laughing. "Mom, you sure are persistent! Like I've said before, you'll find out whether it's a boy or a girl along with everyone else on Christmas Day."

"Well, you can't blame me for trying again but I still feel like I should be given some special provision since I'm your mom," Maddy said.

Hope laughed but then her face looked more serious.

"Mom, can I ask you a question? And don't get upset, please?"

"Of course," Maddy said, puzzled by her daughter's words.

"You how I promised I'd talk to Dad? Well, he called me last night. I told him to leave you alone but he really wants to talk to you. He wouldn't tell me why but promised it wasn't something bad. He even said he ran into you while shopping the day after Thanksgiving. I know things were pretty bad when you got a divorce but that's in the past. Maybe it wouldn't be such a bad idea to talk to him and find out what's going on. Then you can tell him to leave you alone."

Maddy took a deep breath and sighed. How could she explain this to her daughter when, at times, she did not even understand what was going on in her own mind?

"First of all, you sound like Jason. He kinda said the same thing but I'm starting to feel like my old self again. I have this wonderful man in my life that makes me feel so special – something I honestly have never felt before. Not even with your Dad. I'm sorry if that upsets you but you've told me many times that you've never seen me happier." Maddy paused trying to choose her next words carefully.

"Your Dad and I just don't mix. It seemed we couldn't even have decent conversations when we were married, then he wouldn't talk to me at all after he walked out. I was so hurt that I was glad I didn't have to speak to him. But now I've put that behind me and found Jason. I find it odd that suddenly your father wants to talk to me. The whole thing feels, I don't know, strange. I don't have a good feeling about it. I hope you understand."

"I do, in a way, but a part of me wishes the two of you could talk. You could find out what is going on. And you know once the baby is born there will be times you'll probably be running into him like birthday parties and such. But then again, I remember how I felt when he first left. I was mad but once we had that explosive argument, things began to heal. I'm not saying what he did to you or me was right but at least he did apologize to me. Maybe he wants to do the same thing with you? Just a guess because I've tried, subtly, to ask what's going on with him and I get nothing," Hope said contemplatively.

"I'll have to wait and see." Maddy sat there, now uncomfortable, wishing she could have given her daughter a better answer. Instead she could only feel the pain from the past haunting her thoughts once again, something she had sworn she was not going to do anymore.

"Mom, quit scratching your arm."

"What?"

"You look like you are going to scratch your arm off," Hope said.

Maddy pulled up the sleeve of her sweater to see large hives on her arms. She quickly tugged at the collar of her sweater. "Hope do you see any welts on my neck?"

"Yes. Do you need a shot?" Hope asked in a panicked voice.

"No, some Benadryl should do the trick. But if I fall asleep, you'll know why." Maddy reached for her purse and took a double dose of the liquid medicine.

"Mom I'm sorry. Didn't mean to cause you any trouble."

"Sweetheart, you didn't do this. I'm sure it was something I ran into at the store or this cold weather. Sometimes I do wonder if we shouldn't move to the Florida Keys since I was so much better there but then I wouldn't be able to see my grandbaby as much as I want."

Within a few minutes, Maddy could feel the medicine was working, causing her to become drowsy. She drank some more water, which also helped with the reaction. It had to be the stress. The stress of Greg's calls. Of seeing him. Of talking about him. But she chided herself. *You are strong enough to handle this,* she said silently but soon she was fast asleep.

"Hello there, sleepy head," Jason said as Maddy opened her eyes, a little confused. The last thing she remembered was talking to Hope.

"Is Hope already gone?"

"She has been gone awhile. She called me to let me know you had a reaction but that you were fine. After you fell asleep, Shawn picked her up and I've been home for a little over an hour. How are you feeling?"

"Fine, just trying to wake up. Not itching anymore, thank goodness."

"What do you think caused it?" Jason asked, still sitting on the edge of the couch where she lay.

"Who knows," Maddy said with a bit of exasperation in her voice. "I've been doing so good and now I feel like I'm moving backwards. It's all very frustrating. We're supposed to go see the outdoor Christmas movie tonight. Do we still have time to go?"

"I think we need to stay home. Let's just watch something here except I would think you would be sick of those movies by now."

Maddy smiled at him. "I never get tired of Christmas movies. You might as well get used to that."

Jason bent down and gave her a tender kiss. "If it means having you with me, then Christmas movies it is. But as for watching one outdoors, we need to rethink that. We're doing way too much. Maybe that's why you're having reactions."

Maddy sat up. She wanted to prove to him and to herself that she could go. She wanted to share this with him. "Please, let's go. Please?"

Jason had his reservations but she did look fine. Plus, he did like the movie "Elf" and had never before watched it outdoors. "Let me fix a big thermos of coffee and you, my dear, dress very warmly. We'll even bring some extra blankets."

Maddy jumped up, quickly wrapping her arms around her husband. "It won't take me but a few minutes and I'll be ready to go!" and she hurried down the hall.

The little park where the movie was being shown was not too far from the house and they made it in time to have a great spot. The large outdoor screen was bolted tightly to the ground and ready for the movie. There were crowds of people, huddled together, everyone dressed warmly and seeming to have a good time judging by the lively talk and laughter. Everyone also seemed to have piles of blankets to keep them shielded from the unseasonably very cold air. Jason set up their chairs, putting their drinks and food near them then pulled out their own blankets, draping them across the two of them.

"This is certainly different. I've never done this before," Jason said as he looked around. "I'm glad we came."

"Me too," Maddy said as she laid her head on his shoulder. "You're the best husband, you know that, right?"

"Of course," Jason said with a laugh and digging into his coat pockets at the same time.

"Crap! I left my gloves in the car. I should be back before the movie starts. You need anything else?"

"I'm all set."

"I'll be right back."

Maddy watched as her husband walked away, a big smile on her face and in her heart. Her thoughts drifted back to the first day she saw him in the Florida Keys. How she and her best friend, Riley, had talked about the good-looking guy across the street. Maddy sat in the chair, eyes closed, reliving the memory.

"Hey Maddy."

She recognized the voice but there was absolutely no possible way it could be him. But Maddy opened her eyes to see her ex standing near her chair. "Greg, what are you doing here?" she asked calmly though she wanted to scream.

"We always came here every year. I still do. You by yourself?"

"Of course not! Jason has gone to the car for a moment. And if I remember correctly, I had to practically beg you to come to the movie. You only came because Hope wanted to, certainly not because of me. So why are you here now? Haven't seen you here the last three years." Maddy was getting angry. Why this man was so determined to spoil her Christmas was beyond her.

"Did you get my message? I really want to talk to you. Please."

"Greg, there is nothing to say. I mean nothing! Please, please leave me alone. I don't know what you're up to but I have a new life. And I know we'll run into each other because of the grand-baby but please, go live your life, away from me."

"What's going on?" Jason said, a hint of rage radiating from his voice.

"Greg was just leaving," Maddy said forcefully.

"Well that's good to hear," Jason said then turned to Greg. "But I have something to say. Leave my wife alone. She wants nothing to do with you and I promise you don't want to deal with me." Maddy could tell Jason was mad but holding his temper as much as he could.

Greg glanced at Maddy then back at Jason. "Enjoy the movie," was all he said before he turned and left the area.

They both watched him walk away as the movie began but Jason had had enough. "Maddy, if this happens one more time, something has to be done. I'm not sure what but it's almost like he is stalking you. This is crazy."

"I know. I don't want to talk to him but I don't think he is going to leave me alone either."

"Oh yes he will if I have anything to do with it."

Maddy took Jason's hand. "Right now let's watch the movie. I think we both need a little laugh." Maddy wanted to diffuse the situation and enjoy this time with her husband but she could not help feeling that the situation was getting more uncomfortable by the minute. Greg was being very persistent which was so out of character from the man she knew a long time ago.

"But we can't let this go on. I mean, he has come around so much that I'm concerned about your safety now."

"I don't think he would hurt me but it's strange. Let's discuss it tomorrow. I really want to enjoy the movie. Remember, this is one Christmas movie you like."

"True, just frustrated."

"I want to have a bit of fun with you tonight."

"Right here?" Jason said, laughing a bit, trying to diffuse the uneasiness of what had happened.

"What I meant was fun *watching* the movie," Maddy laughed. Jason's words had made her blush. "As for the other, we'll see about that once we get home."

They kept warm under the mountain of blankets Jason had insisted they bring which turned out to be a blessing in the cold night air. They watched the movie, finally laughing and letting go some of the stress that had filled the atmosphere only moments before the movie started. Maddy's mind churned, replaying everything that happened. Plus, she could not help but glance around during the movie to see if Greg was still close by. He was calling too much and showing up at the places he knew she loved to go. Something was definitely amiss and as much as she wanted to act as though none of this existed, she was going to have to find out what was going on with her ex-husband.

7

"A scavenger hunt? Seriously?" Jason said with a smirk on his face.

"They're fun! I've done one every year and it's great. I have this list," Maddy said, showing Jason the piece of paper in her hand, "and all we have to do is visit the local neighborhoods and find the different decorations. Every year, I usually find each one. I've been going by myself for the last few years. Then, as a treat, I go have some French fries at this little restaurant I know where, thank goodness, I haven't had any reactions to their food. It was a bit weird, at first, to do this alone but fun too. Now I can share with my wonderful husband," she said, batting her eyes like a flirting schoolgirl, trying to coerce him into the Christmas spirit. She wanted him to follow her on the next adventure she had planned for the two of them.

Jason only looked at Maddy, smiled and shook his head. He was so tired. The day had been a difficult one on the job site with a delay he was not expecting. On his drive home, all he wanted to do was come home, have some dinner and sit by the fire while he watched TV. But the look on his wife's face was like a little girl in a toyshop. How could he say no?

"If you promise to let me get a big hamburger with bacon, loaded fries and a milk shake, I'll go."

"But that's not healthy!"

"But it's a compromise," Jason said with a grin, eyebrows raised.

Maddy shook her head while laughing. "You have a deal."

"Give me a few minutes to change my clothes and we'll be on our way."

"Yes!" Maddy said excitedly.

They drove around the different neighborhoods on James Island, hunting for specific items, using the flashlight from her phone to illuminate the list on the paper in her hand. Maddy marked off item after item of Christmas decorations they saw in people's yards as they looked at the different holiday displays. Even though Jason was tired, he admitted to himself that the fun of hunting for a particular display such as "Find Mr. and Mrs. Santa Clause" helped him forget the tension of the workday.

"There's Snoopy! We did it! All twenty-five items found and checked off," Maddy said excitedly. "Thanks, this was so much fun." She reached over, hugged her husband then gave him a soft kiss on his earlobe, feeling him shiver slightly at her touch.

"You know I wasn't sure about this but that was fun. Something else I've never done for the holidays though I think we should have combined the scavenger hunt with the Festival of Lights. We would've been finished in no time!" Jason laughed.

"There's no challenge in that!" Maddy said, poking him in the arm.

"But now, it's time for food. I'm starving! Where to?"

Maddy quickly gave him directions to the little diner on the island and before long, the dinner feast they had agreed upon was before them.

"I like this place. We'll have to come back more often, especially since you can eat here," Jason said.

"Hey, don't forget that we are going to the Nutcracker Ballet this weekend," Maddy said as she ate another French Fry.

"I thought this weekend was free because next weekend is Christmas?" Jason said.

"I've planned too much haven't I? I'm sorry. I wanted your first Christmas here to be special. There is so much to do and see."

"Like I told you before - the thing that makes it the most special is that it's my first Christmas with you," Jason said, reaching across the table and gently taking her hand. "And don't take this wrong, but you look a little tired. Do you think that maybe you are over doing it a bit?" Jason said the words gently, knowing that this was hard for Maddy to hear.

"You sure know how to make a girl feel good," Maddy said teasingly but she knew Jason was correct. She did not want to admit it. She had been going non-stop, trying to make this the best holiday ever but even her body was telling her to slow down. "You're right. I don't feel my best but I'm almost afraid to slow down. I want to enjoy the holiday and for it to be special. To do these things with someone that really wants to be with me. Who wants to..."

Tears welled up in Maddy's eyes then began to silently slide down her cheeks. "I've always wanted someone in my life that wanted me in theirs. That I could have long talks with, share my loves and passions. To share everything together even if we enjoy different things. And this Christmas I have you. I guess I'm trying to forget a lot of hurt from the past by doing everything I can with you during these few weeks of the holiday. I don't know – like maybe I'm making up for lost time. I'm really sorry."

Jason reached over and wiped the tears from her cheek. "There is nothing to be sorry about. I knew something was going on but I didn't want to spoil your fun. I want you to be happy but I also want you to be healthy. We don't have to do everything that's available for the season. But we do have tickets to the ballet and we're going to that. So, let's do this. For the rest of the week, we are going to relax. Take it easy. Work on your paintings. I know you have some commission work for next year already and your website is booming. Maybe even finish our Christmas shopping by going online and ordering everything." Jason gave her hand a soft squeeze and looked sweetly into her eyes.

"As far as I'm concerned, my Christmas present is sitting right in front of me. And the best thing is that I get to unwrap her and spend time with her every single day. It doesn't get any better than that in my book." With that, Jason lifted her hand and kiss the back of it. "I love you Maddy Burnett, my best Christmas gift ever."

If Maddy was crying before, it was nothing like now except these were happy tears. "I love you too and I promise to slow down. As for Christmas gifts, they are already done. I do think I'll take your suggestion for painting though. It always seems to relax me and I'll just put some holiday music on in the background."

"That's my girl."

8

The auditorium was filled to capacity as Maddy looked around. She and Jason had excellent seats for the ballet, the same ones she always tried to get for any event she came to at the North Charleston Performing Arts Center. But it had been a while because of her reactions to perfumes and fragrances. For tonight, she had her breathing mask right inside her handbag along with some rescue medicine in case she needed it. Maddy wanted to see the ballet again since it had been a few years since she had attended. She had danced as a child but was never really good at it though she loved every minute of her dance classes. That was about the same time her art teacher handed her some paints with a brush and she found her true creative passion.

As the lights dimmed and the dancers took to the stage, Maddy wrapped her arm through Jason's and sat there mesmerized by the music and the performers. She glanced at Jason to see he was enjoying it and that made her feel good. At first, she thought he was going along just for her but she could tell that Jason was genuinely watching the show. But as the lights came up for an intermission, she was glad.

"Perfect timing because I've got to go to the bathroom," Maddy whispered into Jason's ear, "and someone behind us smells like they drowned themselves in lavender oil instead of taking a bath."

"I smelled that too. Are you okay?" Jason asked.

"Yes, but right now I need to find the restroom."

"I'll go with you."

"That might cause a commotion once we go inside," Maddy teased him.

"Ha, ha. I'll wait for you in the lobby," Jason said as he rolled his eyes.

"You don't have to go. I'll be fine."

"No, I need to stretch my legs and get a drink if the line isn't too long."

The lobby was packed with people and the line to the restroom was long but it didn't matter. She needed the bathroom, even if it meant she missed the beginning of the second act.

By the time Maddy emerged from the restroom, Jason was standing there, waiting for her, with drink in hand. But the person behind him was the one who caught her eyes.

Jason watched as his wife started toward him, a look of fury clearly defining her face. Instead of coming to stand beside him, she passed right by. He turned to see whom she was walking toward and now Jason could feel a sense of outrage inside of himself.

"I've had it!" Maddy said, loud enough to illicit a few stares from people passing by. "You keep calling. You keep showing up wherever I go. I've told you so many times I don't want to talk to you but you can't get that through your thick head."

"Did you ever think that maybe I came to see the show? With someone?" Greg said not raising his voice.

Maddy laughed. "That's a joke. I'd ask you to come with us and your answer was always the same: no. You never came but now all the sudden you love the..." but Maddy stopped mid-sentence. Her breathing was ragged and she felt cold all over. *Not now!* she told herself. But Maddy knew what was happening. Her blood pressure was dropping and she felt like she was going to pass out. But not before she felt strong arms around her.

"Maddy, stay with me. You're okay. I've got your medicine right here." Maddy could hear the voice but it sounded as though it was in the distance.

"Is she ok?" Greg asked.

Jason was more than angry but he didn't have time to answer his question. He laid Maddy on the floor, grabbed her EpiPen from her bag and gave her a shot in the thigh.

"There is an Emergency room right down the street," someone said from behind. Jason looked around to see several people offering help, the security staff running toward them.

"I called 911 and an ambulance is on the way," a woman said as she knelt beside Jason as he laid Maddy on the floor, putting her coat under her head.

"I'm a nurse. Does she have any medical conditions?" the woman asked.

"An illness called Mastocytosis. Causes Anaphylaxis."

"Now I understand the EpiPen."

"Thanks for helping," was all Jason could say. But with a nurse by Maddy's side, Jason suddenly stood up and rushed toward Greg. He wanted to hit him but the two men only stared at each other.

"You son of a bitch! I better never see you near her again. Ever! See what you have done? The pain? The stress? Not just now but in the past. Let her go! And you better hope she is ok," Jason said with venom in his voice then knelt back to his wife as the stretcher was being wheeled into the lobby. When Maddy was safely being tended to by the EMTs, only then did Jason glance back up to see that Greg was nowhere to be found.

Maddy opened her eyes to see the familiar machines around her. It was almost déjà vu from what happened in Florida when she passed out on the steps of her rental home.

"Hey sweetheart," Jason said softly, caressing her cheek with his hand. "Waiting for you to wake up so we can go home. Doctor said you're going to be fine but that you are to rest and drink lots of fluid. You were very dehydrated. I guess that and the perfume factory that was sitting behind us wasn't a great combination for keeping your body from having a reaction. Seems you must have really pissed off your Mast Cells," Jason said trying to bring some levity to the situation.

"I'm really sorry. What happened to Greg?"

"He left but not before me telling him to leave you alone. I guess you could say I threatened him. I came mighty close to hitting him but I was too worried about you. Maddy," Jason said wrapping his hand and arm around hers, "we're going to find out what the hell he's up to. You helped me through all that I had to deal with when Andrea showed back up in my life. Now I can help you."

"Jason, that's just the point. There is no reason for him to be bugging me. Plus, I thought I'd let all that go. That I had forgiven him for all the horrible things he did. But maybe I haven't. I think that's part of the reason I've been on this Christmas overload. I've been trying to create the perfect Christmas that I always wanted but never had. But we aren't perfect. None of us are. What Greg did to Hope and me was terrible but it could've been worse. I've let that past anger overshadow what I have right here in front of me. You." She reached up weakly with her other hand and stroked his face even though she had an IV in the crook of her arm.

"I'm so sorry. But the only way I'm going to heal from this is to talk to him. Not yell. Not scream. But tell him how I feel. How he made me feel. But also listen to what he has to say. Whatever it is, it's important to him. I don't owe him anything like my time but I want to do this for me. I think I have to so I can move on with my life. Because you're right. It's me and you now and I couldn't ask for a better husband or best friend. But like you dealt with Andrea and was able to close that chapter of your life, I need to close this one."

Jason understood. She might be tired but her thinking was clear. He did not want her to have any contact with her ex but she was right. She needed to close the door and he would stand back and let her. He would be there for her no matter what she needed to do.

9

"I can't believe it's almost Christmas," Riley said. "I wish I was there! I would be if Carter's boss hadn't called on him at the last minute. You know we'd be having an all-day pajama party right now."

Maddy laughed as she listened to her best friend and knew she was right. Riley knew how to have a good time no matter what and Maddy wished she did not live so far away. But had it not been for Riley living in Islamorada in the Florida Keys, Maddy might have never met Jason.

"Well, you're going to be here for New Year's Eve and that's something to look forward to."

"How have you been feeling since the other night?" Riley asked.

"Oh, I'm fine. It's been three days but Jason is still making me promise every day that I'll stay at the house and take it easy. He was supposed to be off this week but his project didn't go as planned. Although after today, he's off till after New Year's Day. He says he wants me to rest so we can have the best Christmas. I think it's his way of keeping tabs on me so he doesn't have to worry even though I told him I'm perfectly fine."

"Have you talked to Greg since that night?"

"No but I've been tempted to call. Each time I pick up the phone, though, I can't do it. I've got this perfect conversation all played out in my mind but I hesitate."

"Why?" Riley asked with surprise. "He's an asshole Maddy so don't let him intimidate you. Not again."

"I don't know. It's weird Riley. He was such a big part of my life. We were married for twenty-five years! We have a child together. I don't want to hurt him but I do want him to leave me alone. Well, truthfully, sometimes I want to smack him now that I've seen him again."

"You're worried about hurting him? After everything he did? Sometimes I think you're too soft hearted, Maddy."

"Is that a bad thing?" Maddy asked.

"No, it's actually good but then it can put you in a pickle like you find yourself right now."

The phone began to beep and Maddy looked at it to see it was a call coming from Shawn. "Riley, I have to go. Shawn is calling in. Probably something about Christmas presents because I know he's been trying to figure out what to get Hope for Christmas. I'll call you later."

"Take care of yourself and love ya! See you New Year's Eve and can't wait for a party at the beach," Riley said before hanging up the phone.

"Hi Shawn," Maddy said as the phone call transferred over to him.

"Hi Maddy." Shawn's voice was faltering putting Maddy instantly on alert.

"What's going on Shawn?"

"We're at the hospital. Hope didn't want me to call but I think she might need you."

"What happened?" Maddy could feel her heartbeat speeding up as she listened to Shawn.

"Hope was having a bit of a problem with her blood sugar this morning. Then it went too low and she ended up in the ER. Now they are saying that the baby might be in distress. Plus, she is bleeding a little." Maddy could tell that Shawn was trying to stay calm but she could hear the concern in his voice.

"I'm on my way. She is at the Medical University, right?" Maddy asked getting up, grabbing her coat and handbag.

"Yes. Thanks, Maddy," Shawn said and the phone clicked off.

Maddy was in her car quickly, not bothering to change from her blue jeans and sweatshirt. She only knew she had to get to the hospital. As she drove, every second was bringing back so many memories of Hope and the times when Maddy would have to rush her to the emergency room. Maddy would be so scared, wondering if something bad was about to happen, if she was about to lose her only child, unable to see any positive thing around her. And like it was right now, in those same memories, she always seemed to be by herself.

"Hey there! Are you resting like I hope you said you would?" Jason said happily as he answered the phone.

"Jason," Maddy said, doing her best to hold back the tears, "Hope is in the hospital. She and the baby are having complications and I'm on my way there now. I wanted to let you know."

"Give me a few minutes and I'm on my way. I'll meet you there. Be careful and call me when you find out something. But Maddy, please take care of yourself. Did you take everything you needed?"

"I have some snacks in my handbag along with my medicine." And then she laughed. "If I do need any help, I'm at a hospital."

"I'll be there as quick as I can."

"Thank you, Jason. I love you."

"I love you too."

Maddy began wiping the tears that she suddenly could not hold back. This is supposed to be a wonderful time of the year. Why now were there so many obstacles? Why so many harsh realities hitting them all at once?

She knew there was one call that she needed to make and a horrible feeling came over her. Maddy dialed Greg's number and was a bit relieved when no one answered. So, she left a message telling Hope's father the situation. If the past was any indicator, he might show up, he might not. Maddy would have to wait and see.

"Hi there baby girl," Maddy said as she took the chair beside Hope's hospital bed. Though her daughter looked pale, Maddy could still see the twinkle in her eyes. That spark that had always let her know in the past that her little girl was a fighter.

"Seems like my granddaughter is trying to come a bit early," Maddy said softly.

"I'm still not telling you till Christmas," Hope said with a weak voice and a smile on her face.

"Once again, you can't blame me for trying." Maddy reached over the bed rail and stroked her daughter's hair, so reminiscent of the hospital stays of Hope's childhood. It seemed to soothe both mother and daughter at the same time. It was usually just the two of them and Maddy always felt like it was them against the world. This time was different. Now it was both of them along with Maddy's grandchild that would fight the circumstances. She sat quietly and prayed that both Hope and the baby would fight like never before.

"I saw that Shawn had fallen asleep so I took the liberty of talking to your doctor and nurse. Seems your sugar is back in normal range but you are still bleeding. Hopefully they will find out soon what is going on."

"Momma, I can't lose my baby," Hope whispered, still so weak from everything that had happened. Tears were sliding down her face and onto the pillow forming a wet puddle.

"You aren't going to," Maddy said. "It's Christmas and this is the time for miracles. You're strong and always have been so I know this grandchild of mine if a fighter like you. But you do need your rest so why don't you close your eyes."

"I know I'm going to sound like a little kid but will you stay right here? Hold my hand till I fall asleep like you did when I was younger?"

Maddy reached through the bed railing and clasped her daughter's hand.

"Rest now. That way you can come home for Christmas, okay?"

"I love you Momma."

"I love you too baby."

Maddy watched as Hope closed her eyes and the scene before her felt like so many of the other times they found themselves in the hospital for Hope or now for herself. The machines in the room. The smell of the hospital. Even the ride up in the elevator had Maddy in a nervous knot. She had to keep it together for her daughter. Hope needed her again, like she had all those times growing up. But Maddy felt good knowing that her daughter now had Shawn. He was Hope's rock even if Hope still asked for her mother.

Hope's breathing was soon in a steady rhythm, indicating she was finally sleeping, something Maddy knew, from much experience, would help. She only prayed that they would find out the cause of the bleeding and that it would stop. Though the baby could be born right now and possibly survive, Maddy did not want that for her grandchild.

"Maddy, can I come in?" She heard Jason's whispered voice and it was like music to her ears. She got up and before he was completely in the door, her arms were wrapped around his neck, not letting him move. Maddy's tears were silent but left wet spots on Jason's shirt.

"It's going to be alright," Jason whispered as he held his wife softly. "This is just a bump in the road. Any news?"

Maddy quietly filled him in on everything she knew. Hope and Shawn were both still sleeping so they decided to walk to the waiting room. It was spacious with windows that gave them a perfect view of the city surrounding them. Maddy stood there, looking outside as the sun was starting to set.

"Jason, I really thought this Christmas was going to be so special. You know, our first Christmas together. I had so many things planned. Things that I always wanted to share with someone but really never got the chance before now. It seemed like there was always something going on, someone sick or an argument that would ruin whatever I had planned. I felt like it would be different this year. Since I met you, everything seemed so, I don't know, perfect. Magical. I sound silly but I wanted a normal, happy Christmas."

"Maddy, what's normal?" Jason looked at her then took a seat on the couch that lined the wall, patting the spot beside him for her to sit with him. It was only the two of them in the quiet room.

"Normal is Christmas parades, lights on pretty trees, holiday movies, shopping for gifts. Listening to Christmas music. Lots of family together, opening gifts on Christmas day. Holiday dinners. Fireworks on New Year's Eve. It's certainly not ER visits. Not my pregnant baby girl fighting for her life and our grandchild's. Not dealing with an ex-husband." Maddy felt like she wanted to scream but was doing her best to keep her emotions calm.

"Think about what you have told me. We have looked at lights. Had a scavenger hunt. Saw part of a ballet. Went to the light festival. Watched more Christmas movies than I can count! And I can't listen to one radio station without hearing holiday music. Hell, one station here is nothing but that! Instead of striving for perfect what about us enjoying what we have - each other. A beautiful family with a grandchild on the way. We can enjoy the beach whenever we want. You're a successful artist. You're the best wife along with your other very pleasant attributes." Jason had tried to elicit a smile and when Maddy looked up there was a slight grin on her face.

"Once again, the most important thing is that we have each other. I know schedules have been a bit crazy and it's not what you'd planned but I've loved my Christmas with you so far. When Hope is out of the hospital and if you stay on good behavior, opening gifts is going to be quite fun. Then on New Year's Eve, Riley and Carter are going to be here and we're going to have one hell of a fireworks display." By now Maddy was wrapped up in Jason's arms, finally releasing some of the tension that had built up from the day.

"You're right. I've been like a crazy woman trying to do every little thing that involves Christmas instead of being in the moment and taking in all the blessings around us. I definitely didn't want it to be this stressful."

"Can you ever tell me a Christmas season, even when we were kids, that didn't involve a little bit of stress?" Jason laughed.

Maddy could not help but laugh too. "You're right yet again. How did you get to be so smart?"

"I think it was when I married you," and Jason tenderly kissed her lips as he caressed the side of her face.

They heard someone clear their throat only to look up and see Greg standing in the room. Jason felt Maddy's body tense up as she sat up straighter.

"Hi. I guess you got my message."

"Thanks for calling me. I went in her room and she was sleeping. That's when the nurse told me you were here."

"Jason, if you don't mind, I need to talk to Greg for a moment," Maddy said looking at Jason with a smile. Then she whispered. "I think it's time he and I had a chat."

"Are you sure you are up to this right now?" Jason whispered.

"I think so."

"I'll be out in the hall if you need me," Jason said, squeezing her hand for a bit of encouragement. He walked by Greg, giving him a look of warning, and left the room.

10

"Is it okay for me to sit down?" Greg said, motioning to the chair in front of the couch where Maddy sat.

"Of course," Maddy said in a monotone voice trying to keep her senses in tack and not let this man jumble her thoughts. She knew what she wanted to say to Greg but she also knew she had to listen to him first to find out what was exactly going on

"How is Hope doing?" Greg asked.

"Her blood sugar is under control, but she's bleeding. They haven't come back yet with any other news but all I know is it's too early for the baby to be born. So, we're waiting to hear from the doctors."

Greg sat across from her, shaking his head as he stared at the floor.

"Greg, you have been calling me for almost a month now. You've shown up at places I haven't seen you at in years. Why, after all this time, do you need to talk to me so badly?"

Greg finally looked up but not at Maddy. He stared out the window that was now dark. "I screwed up."

Maddy looked at him, trying to understand what he was talking about. "Okay. That's it?"

"Maddy, I made a mistake. Well, actually, I've made a ton of mistakes. I can look back now and see I really messed up. And losing you was the biggest mistake of all." Greg stood up and came to sit beside her but Maddy scooted down the couch a bit further.

"I know you're married now and this is going to sound crazy, but I still love you. I want you to be a part of my life again. I know I can be a better man. These last three years made me realize what an asshole I was to you and Hope. I want to change that. I want to prove to both of you that I'm not that person any more. I just need another chance."

Maddy was shocked by the words she was hearing. Was he serious? He knew she was married but he had the audacity to say he still loved her and wanted her back?

"Greg, first of all, I can't believe what I'm hearing. You have the nerve to say you want me back? I'm married! And truly happy for the first time in as long as I can remember!" Maddy tried to keep her voice as unruffled as she could but it was proving to be difficult.

"Maddy, I know now I really love you. I need you back in my life," Greg said more passionately.

"Didn't you just hear me? Jason is my life now, not you."

"You've haven't been together that long. What - a few months? We were married twenty-five years. That should count for something," Greg said looking at her with desperate eyes. "I know we can make it work. You need to give me another chance."

Maddy sat stunned. Was she truly hearing these words from this man that had wronged her in so many ways?

"Do you know how ridiculous you sound? I actually can't believe what I'm hearing. I thought you wanted to talk to me about maybe an apology, or long-lost property we once had or something we didn't settle during the divorce. But a declaration of love? And here at the hospital with your daughter down the hall fighting for herself and our grandchild? You're truly crazy! But then why should things be any different from before? Any time Hope went to the hospital growing up you were hardly there or flirting with the nurses. Didn't seem concerned about your daughter but only yourself, like now."

"Dammit Maddy, I just told you I screwed up and I want you back in my life. Want to be married to you then everything will be alright. Life will be like it's supposed to be." Greg tried to scoot closer to her but this time Maddy quickly stood up.

"You're serious? Have you listened to yourself or to anything I've said? I'm married to the sweetest man I know. He's not only my husband but also my best friend. He loves me, wants to be with me no matter what. I've never known love like this before. I don't say these things to hurt you but to let you know there is no chance for you and me. It's hard for me to sit here and comprehend that you even think that I would consider leaving my husband.

"Just because your two marriages have ended in divorce doesn't mean mine will. Not by a long shot. But we were over the day you walked out on me and then when you finally admitted to the affair so you could move the divorce along more quickly. No, actually it was even before all of that.

"You were hardly there when Hope would end up in the hospital. When she was sick, it was me who took care of her. Then I was sick, you acted as though it was all in my head. I had no help from you whatsoever. The cruel things you said. Your time was spent in front of a TV screen getting upset if I mention any kind of family time. It didn't matter to you. I thought if I kept trying, doing everything I could think of to make you happy that you would be more of a husband. But you didn't. Then I started to blame myself thinking I wasn't good enough. And when I got sicker, you walked out! You didn't care!" Maddy was mad now.

As hard as she was trying to keep it together, his words that he wanted her back appalled her and made her sick to her stomach.

"I wanted to talk to you about this somewhere else. Not at the hospital," Greg said, keeping a quiet demeanor.

"It doesn't matter where we talk, you're out of your mind! I can't believe you have said all this! I can't say this enough: you're insane!" Maddy could not keep from saying what she was truly thinking. All her resolve to be calm and nice had gone out the window the moment Greg had the audacity to say he loved her.

"Maddy, I know it sounds odd but I've had a lot of time for some soul searching. And I know you're the only one for me. I've changed. Ask Hope. I'm working. Spending time with my family, even more time with Hope. I'm not sleeping around. I'm not even dating. All I have been thinking about is you."

"Me? For goodness sakes, Greg, you've been married twice in three years! You sound like a desperate man to me. I'm not the consolation prize in your life." Maddy started to feel light headed and knew she was hyperventilating. She slowly sat back down in the chair away from Greg and took slow, deep breaths to get this under control. The last thing she needed was to end up in the ER again.

"Maddy, will you at least give it some thought?"

"I thought you had something reasonable to talk about but I was sorely mistaken.

You have lost your mind! I'll say this one more time so listen - leave me alone," Maddy said. She stood quickly, not giving him another glance and began to walk out of the room.

"Please, just think about it. You know I'm right," Greg said but Maddy continued toward the door and out to the hall. She headed toward Hope's room but was dizzy. Then she felt a pair of strong, familiar hands on her arm.

"Hey, what happened? What did he say? Are you ok?" Jason said immediately taking Maddy in his arms and holding her. She responded by hugging him as tightly as she could and squeezing her eyes shut to keep tears of rage from falling.

"What happened? I started hearing your voice and was about to come back in there," Jason asked, desperately wanting to know the circumstances since Maddy was in such a state.

"Right now, I need to go check on Hope. I can't talk about it here."

"Okay," Jason said concerned.

To Maddy's surprise, when she opened the door to her daughter's hospital room, Hope was sitting in bed, eating some Jell-O. Shawn was now awake and going through the channels available on the hospital TV.

"I thought you two would still be sleeping," Maddy said as she came to stand by her daughter's bed, keeping her composure as best she could.

"Hey there girl! You trying to give your Momma a scare?" Jason said in a lighthearted tone then bent over to give Hope a kiss on the top of her head.

The hospital door opened once more behind them and Greg stepped into the room. Maddy kept a smile on her face for Hope's sake but she wanted to run out of the room as she saw him standing on the other side of Hope's hospital bed.

"Hey Dad," Hope said. "How did you know I was here?"

"Your Mom left me a message. Any news?"

"The doctor just left. My sugar is doing fine but they want me to stay here for a few days to be on the safe side. The bleeding is slowing down and they think everything is fine but I will be on strict bed rest till the baby is born. That's another nine weeks unless the baby comes early which I pray doesn't happen. But nine weeks? I'm going to go stir crazy!"

"Then we'll have plenty of pajama days, watch movies, maybe paint, color – whatever. I know we planned Christmas at our house but we'll officially move it to yours. Don't worry about a thing. We'll take care of everything so you and Shawn can relax. We want a healthy baby and momma in a few months. Plus, we want you home for Christmas. I think that's the best present ever," Maddy said as she took the seat beside Hope then leaned over and hugged her daughter.

"Well, I'm going to take your Momma home. I think she needs a bit of rest herself," Jason said.

"Yes, she does. We've been here quite a few times over the years and I know how hard it is on her. But Shawn is here for me. So, Momma," Hope said as she looked at Maddy, "go home and rest. I'll stay on my best behavior to make sure we get to come home soon. We'll talk on the phone tomorrow and make plans for Christmas dinner. And Dad," Hope said looking at Greg, "I've wanted to call you to make sure you'd come to Christmas dinner as well. We have the big announcement about the baby and we want you all to be there."

Maddy's body felt a little limp at Hopes' words. In all the excitement about the holidays, Maddy had forgotten about the possibility that her ex would be at the Christmas dinner. If Hope only knew what her father had asked Maddy only moments before, she would have never had both of her parents in the same room. But Maddy did not say anything, only smiled. She was not about to let her ex-husband ruin hers or anyone's Christmas.

"I'll check on you tomorrow. If anything comes up, you call me. I don't care what time it is, alright? Shawn, make her promise she'll call," Maddy said emphatically.

"Maddy, I'll call you if she doesn't but the doctor sounded as though she felt it was going to be okay as long as Hope did as she was told."

"Very good. Then you, my dear, please listen to the doctor and we'll talk tomorrow," Maddy said as she gave her daughter another hug before heading out toward the door.

"I'm going to visit for a few minutes. Talk to you later Maddy. Jason," Greg said, tipping his head toward him.

As they headed to the elevator, Maddy's legs were weak. Everything that had occurred today - Hope, the baby, and Greg's insane request - were about all she could take.

"Maddy what happened back in that room?" Jason said as soon as the elevator doors closed.

"Can we talk about it when we get home? I'm not feeling good and want to get home. I want to take a hot shower and then lay with you on the couch, just the two of us."

"Are you able to drive?" Jason asked concerned.

"I think so. I'll follow you."

"We can always come and get your car tomorrow. I'm off now until after the New Year, remember?"

Maddy had forgotten and felt a big sense of relief wash over her. "Then I'm riding home with you."

As they pulled out of the parking garage, Maddy scooted across the bench seat and sat as close to Jason as she could.

"Maddy, can you talk about it now?" Jason asked once more.

Maddy sat there, staring straight ahead. "He actually told me he wants me to give him another chance and leave you."

11

"Holy shit! Are you serious? Those were his exact words? He does know we're married, not just dating, right? I mean, he knows that! He has to know that." Jason was stunned, repeating his words over and over.

"Oh, he knows and I told him again to make sure there was no doubt. It's so strange. He claims to be a changed man and how sorry he is for what happened during our marriage. That we'd be better together now. That he needs me. That he will take care of me. He sounded so desperate. I couldn't believe what I was hearing. I don't know if he has changed or not, but this is so out of character for him and very odd. I can't talk to Hope about this, not with everything that she is going through with herself and the baby. But Greg kept saying he was sorry for being such an ass all those years. How he treated me and Hope so badly."

"But Maddy, does he think you'd leave me?"

"I actually think he does. He said you and I hadn't been together that long whereas he and I had twenty-five years of marriage. He sounded as though that was more important. Jason, I was so unnerved and I lost my cool. I was so mad, I almost wanted to hit him!"

"Probably should have!" Jason said, feeling so angry that he wanted to turn the truck around and find the man. "I take that back. I need to go back there and beat the shit out of him."

"I made it very clear that you were my husband and I wasn't going anywhere. I'm wondering if he is pulling some stunt to ruin Christmas for me. It wouldn't be the first time." Maddy leaned her head on Jason's shoulder. She could feel the trembling in his body and knew he was as upset as she felt.

"Jason, no one can take me away from you. I even told Greg that this was the happiest I'd ever been. That you are my one and only and always will be."

"I've never doubted your love for me but I do wonder about his tactics. Why this? Why now?"

"Well, it seems we'll be seeing him Christmas Day so maybe I can have a little heart to heart conversation with him once I've calmed down. Make sure this subject is completely closed. I want nothing to do with the man again."

As they pulled into the driveway, the Christmas tree lights had come on while they were gone and it was a welcomed sight to see. It had been a long day filled with stress and anxiety. Right now all Maddy wanted to do was cuddle up in her husband's arms and relax.

Maddy woke to the smell of breakfast the next morning and smiled. *I could get used to this,* she thought as she remembered that Jason was off work for the holidays. But it only took seconds for her to recall the events of yesterday. If Greg was smart, he would leave her alone. As far as she was concerned, his conversation had been absurd. Greg was only in her life because of Hope and she would make that clear.

They made a quick visit to check on Hope when they went to pick up Maddy's car and found out some great news. Hope was being allowed to go home instead of a longer hospital stay but with very strict orders from the doctor. This meant she would definitely be home for Christmas which was music to Maddy's ears. She had spent a Christmas in the hospital with Hope once before and though the staff was great, there was nothing like being at home during the holidays.

"Do you need us to do anything?" Maddy asked her daughter before she and Jason walked out the door.

"Be at the house Christmas Day with bells on," Hope laughed.

"Don't you need someone to stay with you the next few days?" Maddy asked.

"Shawn's off from work until after Christmas," Hope said, taking her husband's hand.

"And what about Christmas dinner?"

"Shawn's Mom is fixing everything and bringing it over Christmas morning. Said that we could heat things up and fix everything around noon. She won't let any of us help. I think she wanted to make it a Christmas breakfast instead of dinner. She is as anxious as you about learning the baby's gender," Hope said smiling.

"Then I'll call your Mom, Shawn, to see if I need to make something," Maddy said then looked to her daughter once more. "I'll come stay with you if you need me to."

"We'll be fine Momma but thanks," Hope said, looking at Shawn who was sitting on the end of her hospital bed. "Kinda weird huh? Before it was always you and me. And now I have Shawn."

"Yeah, but this is a good kinda weird," Maddy said. All these years of taking care of Hope and now her daughter had someone else to help. Maddy was happy but it felt strange. But she also had a new man to take care of her and that felt perfect. If only Maddy could talk to Hope about her dad and the unusual conversation. Maybe her daughter could shed some light on what had been said but she would not burden Hope right now. Her health and that of the baby was more important and Maddy knew, one way or the other, she would figure out this situation.

"So. I'll meet you at home?" Maddy asked, as she and Jason started to head in separate directions to their vehicles.

"Sounds good. Maybe tonight we can take it easy? Watch some regular TV or maybe something more fun?" Jason said.

Maddy smiled at her mischievous husband. "We'll talk about that at home."

The church was crowded for the Christmas Eve service but Jason and Maddy found two seats together on the back row. Though Maddy did not want a repeat of her emergency room visit during the ballet and being in such a crowded space probably was not the best idea, she felt like she was exactly where she needed to be. Hearing the Christmas songs, listening to the holiday message and sitting, contemplating on all that had happened over the last few weeks had her searching her soul. She felt intuitively that Hope and the baby would be okay. The one situation in her life that was not settled had to do with Greg.

Whether Maddy liked it or not, Greg would always be in her life because of their daughter. As she stood with the rest of the congregation, lighting tiny candles, she began to watch the flame before her. All this time, she had thought she had let him go. The moment they had left the courthouse and she and Greg walked opposite ways, Maddy remembered sitting in her car, crying, knowing that their divorce would be good for her future but that it was going to take some time to heal.

At that time, she truly wished Greg would find whatever he was looking for. Maddy had said a prayer that day to forgive him for everything he had done. Then she thought she had let him go and embraced her new future. Though it hurt, she was at peace with what had happened or so she thought. But Greg's calls, appearances and now the talk at the hospital was undoing all that she thought she had come to terms with three years ago. But after all that had happened recently, Maddy realized that she was still holding on to a lot of anger and hurt.

When she blew out the flame of the tiny candle in her hand, Maddy felt as though she had released a burden. She felt peaceful and realized that by admitting to herself that she was still angry, she could now let go of it and the hurt she had been carrying. Yes, things had been bad but that was behind her and the man sitting beside her was her present and her future. Maddy felt like this time she had truly forgiven Greg for how he had treated her all those years.

Even with his insane antics over the last few weeks, Maddy did not feel so much anger anymore but felt sorry for him instead. All the things Greg had said and done were in the past for good now. She did not have to bring them up anymore. If he was at all sincere in what he told her that night at the hospital, and if he was truly sorry for how he had treated her and Hope, then she could forgive him and move on. Actually, it didn't matter if he was sorry or not, Maddy thought. She was choosing to forgive him and let the past go. It would not hold her prisoner any more. The big thing would be to let him know.

Maddy knew now that she had to have another conversation with Greg. To calmly let him know that her future was with Jason and not him. She would speak to him tomorrow, sometime, at Hope's house after they celebrated Christmas. Maddy only hoped with all her heart that he would understand and that this riff, this madness, this hurt, this anger that had been between them would be healed the best it could so Greg could move on in love just like she was now.

"That was a beautiful service," Jason said quietly as they got ready to leave the church.

"It really was," Maddy said, lost in thought.

"Are you okay?" Jason asked.

"Actually, I am but I need to go to the bathroom before we leave."

"No problem. I'll wait right here for you."

There were only a few people waiting in line and Maddy took her phone out to make sure Hope had not called. But she was not expecting the text she had waiting in her messages.

"I just wanted to tell you once more how much I love you. I know things weren't the best but I promise that it will be better than ever now. I'm a new man. You just need to give me another chance. We can start all over. Love Greg."

"Are you okay? Look a bit pale there. If it's Hope you're thinking about, you know she's going to be fine. She's got great doctors and has a wonderful mom. The perfect tonic for what ails any kid," Jason said and kissed Maddy as they walked to the car.

Maddy was quiet, not knowing what to say. She had just experienced a sense of peace about Greg and then reading the text message unnerved her again but this time it was different.

"Something's wrong. I can see it on your face and you're not talking," Jason said with concern.

"I have something to show you when we get in the car."

Once they were seated and warm, Maddy handed her phone to Jason to let him read the message.

"Maddy, this guy is crazy! This shows he is stalking you. You have to let me talk to him tomorrow and stop this."

"I'm going to talk to Greg. Just him and me. I was so angry the other night but now I'm not. Jason, as crazy as this might sound, I want him to find happiness like I have. I know you might not understand after everything Andrea put you through but I hope you do."

"Listen, the situation between my ex-wife and your ex-husband are totally different. She broke the law. Big time! There was nothing I could do to help her and she wouldn't let me. I know the things Greg has done and I can't say that sometimes I just want to – ah, never mind. Let's just say I get very protective of you. But Maddy, you have such a tender heart and I know you only want what is best. I also know that this is as much for you as it is for him, right?"

Her husband could read her so well. "What better time than Christmas to set someone free? My ex and me. Whether he chooses freedom that will be up to him. But for me, it's one of the Christmas presents I have received already this season and it feels so good except that new text message lets me know that I have to clear this up once and for all. Thanks for understanding."

Heading toward home, Jason turned the radio came on. "Have Yourself A Merry Little Christmas" was playing and Maddy felt like the words were written for her at this very moment. She had been dreading the celebration at Hope's house tomorrow but now was actually looking forward to it. It was time for happiness and peace. For her and Jason. And Greg.

12

"Merry Christmas," Jason whispered in her ear. Maddy's eyes opened slowly to see the little tree in their room was already turned on, lights blinking and the fireplace was glowing.

"Merry Christmas to you," she said, reaching up to give her husband, finding his lips to begin their special day. Their first Christmas together and she could not wait.

"It's only going to be in the low 50's today and a bit rainy so make sure to dress to keep warm. But I didn't know if you were ready to get up or wanted to lie in bed a while longer. I do know that Santa has left some gifts under the tree," Jason said with a huge grin on his face.

Maddy sat up, stretched and quickly put on her slippers and fuzzy robe. "I know Santa stopped by because I checked it out last night."

"You went right to sleep while we were watching 'Home Alone'," Jason said in surprise.

"Yes, but I couldn't sleep when I woke up a little later so I went to sit by the Christmas tree. Then I spied some presents for me and you."

"Then what are we waiting for," Jason said like a little kid causing Maddy to follow quickly behind him, both of them laughing like children.

They sat on the floor in front of the tree, the fireplace warming the room. Maddy's first gift from Jason was a beautifully framed picture of the two of them from their wedding day. Riley had sent him some sand from Anne's Beach and a few shells from the Keys that were placed neatly inside the enclosed picture case. It was perfect and Maddy could not wait to find the best place in their beach home to hang the wonderful photo collage.

Jason opened his gift that felt like nothing but an empty box as Maddy giggled. But the note and card inside made him smile then say "No way! You really don't mind?"

"Merry Christmas," Maddy said, reaching over on her hands and knees to kiss him sweetly for the second time this morning.

"I told you that wall would be perfect for a TV of that size. Man, I've always wanted one but have never been in one place long enough. Thanks babe," Jason said, scooting closer to his wife. "Our very own home theater."

They shared other gifts, both of them going just a bit overboard with it being their first holiday together but one gift brought tears to Maddy's eyes. It was a piece of paper with a picture.

"This is really ours?" she said, a smile mixed with happy tears.

"Yep, and whenever you are ready to go and fix it up, we can be on our way. I figured that we should wait till after the baby is born but now, we have our own house in the Florida Keys. Riley was a big help when I was looking even though our place isn't as close to hers as I wanted it to be. It won't be like walking down the street but I'm sure, when you're there, you two will be inseparable."

"I can't wait for the family to come down. Jason, this place is huge. And on the beach. We have our own private beach?" Maddy asked as she studied the pictures.

"Yes, we do," Jason said as he snuggled up beside his wife as they sat on the floor, examining the photo. The lights of the tree were reflecting on her face, giving her a soft, beautiful glow.

"I love you. Not because of the house and the gifts, which are completely wonderful but because you are the most caring, thoughtful person. A best friend. I got so lucky the day I met you. The hunky man Riley and I talked about that was renting the house across the street from me." Maddy kissed him this time with so much passion that before she knew it, they were both lying almost under the tree, lost in the feel of each other.

Jason rolled to his side as he looked down at Maddy. "Now this is what I call the best Christmas gift," he whispered as he began nuzzling her neck, kissing it softly. The small kisses were now starting to trail down to her shoulders as Jason pulled back the top of her robe, sending a tingle throughout her body. Merry Christmas indeed!

"Are you ready for this?" Jason asked as Maddy stood beside the car at Hope's house.

"I think so. Hopefully I can clear up this situation. Only hate to have this conversation on Christmas Day."

"You could always wait. It doesn't have to be today. But then it might be good to get things settled so he knows exactly how you feel. I'll be on standby in case you need me, okay?"

"Thanks, but I think it'll be okay."

"Then let's put on our holiday faces and have some fun, even though he'll be here."

"Oh, I plan to. We get to find out the baby's gender today. Then I can start shopping."

Jason hugged Maddy once again before they started walking toward the front door. "You're so cute when you get excited."

"Merry Christmas everyone," Maddy said as they walked into the house. Hope and Shawn's home was beautifully decorated and Maddy immediately saw her daughter comfortably sitting in the lounger, feet propped up and everything she would need surrounding her: a drink, food, the remote and it looked like some leftover Christmas wrapping paper at her feet.

"Hey, baby, Merry Christmas. You feeling okay today?" Maddy asked as she hugged her daughter.

"Yep but this staying still and resting rule is already driving me crazy. Poor Shawn is having to do everything," Hope said a little defeated.

"And I don't mind," Shawn said loudly from the other room. "Maddy please tell her, again, that she has to listen to doctor's orders."

"I don't think I need to tell you," Maddy said, looking at her daughter. "Between you and me, we know when it's in our best interest to listen, right?"

As Hope rubbed her large abdomen, she nodded her head "yes".

"Look what I got for Christmas," Hope said, extending her hand toward her mom. It was a ring with two colorful stones and an empty facet in the middle. "That," Hope pointed on the ring, "is for when the baby is born. The birthstone will go there."

"Oh, Hope, it's beautiful."

"Shawn is definitely spoiling me. I also got my new computer! Now I have something to play with while I wait for the baby. Maybe even catch up with work a little bit."

The doorbell rang and Maddy started to shake with anticipation of Greg's arrival but it was Shawn's parents with the Christmas dinner. Maddy helped, trying to calm herself for the inevitable conversation that would be coming up this afternoon. She had not talked to Greg since that night at the hospital but remembering the text message last night made her jittery. But she did not have to wait for long. Only a few minutes passed before Greg was walking through the door, presents in hand.

Greg locked eyes with Maddy, smiled then went over to see his daughter. Maddy continued to help Shawn's mom prepare the dinner even though they all determined that Christmas gifts would be first on the agenda of Christmas Day activities.

As they sat in the family room, around the Christmas tree, Hope started. "I know you've all been waiting very patiently to find out if we're having a boy or a girl. So, here we go." Shawn handed each grandparent a bag of M&M's.

"Now on the count of three, open your bag of candy," Hope said.

"How are M&M's going to tell us the sex?" Maddy asked.

"You'll see. Trust me," Hope said with a smile. "Okay, one, two, three!"

They all tore open the bags and dumped into their hands beautiful pink M&M's that said, in tiny writing, "It's A Girl!"

"I knew it!" Maddy said out loud at the same time as Shawn's mom. "A girl! I can't wait to go shopping. A girl! What about names?"

"We're still working on that," Shawn said looking at Hope as he sat on the edge of the chair, holding her hand. "We won't wait so long to give you the news on that one."

For the next thirty minutes, it was an exchange of gifts, thank-yous, hugs and kisses. The atmosphere in the room was warm and filled with the holiday spirit but every time Maddy saw Greg or he even spoke, she felt her nerves heighten.

"Hey," Maddy said quietly as she came up to Greg, "I was wondering if we could talk. Outside on the porch."

"Sure," Greg said smiling.

Before she walked out the door, she looked at Jason who gave her a worried expression but she went out the front door following her ex-husband.

"Merry Christmas," Greg said as he took a seat on the porch swing, patting the seat beside of him for Maddy to sit. Instead, she took a seat in the rocking chair across from him.

"So, I guess I should start. Greg, I'm sorry but all this nonsense has to stop. And now."

"What?"

Maddy looked at him incredulously. "The calls. The texts. Everything. You really can't be serious about all of this?"

"I'm very serious Maddy. I want you back in my life. Even if I have to beg, I know now that you're the only woman for me. I love you and I always have."

Maddy took a deep breath, trying to stay calm. "Greg, it will never happen. I'm very happily married and I would never leave Jason. You may not want to hear this but I really feel like Jason saved my life. He is a part of me I never knew existed. He is the love of my life. I've made that so clear that I don't understand why you won't accept it and move on."

Greg stood up, sighed and hung his head. "I was such a stupid shit. I think back to all the dumb things I did and said. The times when you needed me and I wasn't there. I was like some irresponsible kid that didn't want to grow up. But I've changed," Greg said passionately.

"But why in the world would you think that I'd leave my husband?"

Greg finally looked at her. "After my last divorce, I felt so messed up. For the first time, I really started thinking about my life. I'm fifty-two years old. I can't keep wandering around. Job to job. Person to person. I'm so sorry about what happened over the years and I want to make it right. I thought we could start over again."

"I'm sorry. That's over and done. I'm happy now with Jason," Maddy said.

"I just – I don't know. Like I said, I've done some things I'm not proud of. I just thought," but Greg did not get to finish his words.

"Our marriage is over. Actually, it was over before you walked out when you think about it. But I can tell you this. I honestly forgive you for all the messed-up things that happened when we were married. Neither of us were perfect. I thought that I had let all that hurt go when our divorce was final but with you constantly showing up places, trying to call me and even the text message last night let me know I was still so angry with you. But now, I'm truly over it. I'm letting it all go and I hope you will too."

"So, you don't see any chance for us at all?" Greg said.

"Again, I don't say this to hurt you in any way, but I love Jason more than anyone before. You always hear those words about a soul mate? Well, he is mine. He is my best friend. He is always there for me. For Hope. Jason is truly a wonderful man and I love him very deeply." Maddy watched, as Greg's eyes seem to glaze over, almost as though he was tuning her out.

"Man, I feel like an idiot," Greg said, sitting back in the porch swing, running his hand through his hair and sighed. "For some reason I thought that maybe you'd come back to me. You seem different than when we were married. I really thought I could convince you to give me another chance."

"I am different. I've grown into my own person. I'm not just someone's wife or daughter or mother. I found me. I think you need to do the same thing."

"I've been such a screw up for so long I don't even know where to begin."

"Start by being with yourself. Not finding another woman. That won't fix your problems. I think that's the only reason you keep telling me that you want another chance. Think about it. You don't really love me like a man should love a wife. You want a chance to make up for past mistakes. You can do that without being in a relationship. It starts by changing yourself." Maddy stood up, went to sit beside her ex-husband and for the first time did not feeling repelled by being close to him. "You can't look to a woman or another person to fix what's bothering you. I'm no therapist but it looks like that's what you've been doing since you and I divorced. I think you don't really want me back in your life as a wife. You want someone to fix things for you and no one can. That's up to you."

Greg took a deep breath. There was a silence between them for a few minutes as he seemed to contemplate all that Maddy had said.

"All I can say right now is that Jason is one lucky man. I truly didn't know what I had when we were together."

"Greg, I promise you that there is a woman out there who is perfect for you. That woman is going to see you and know you are meant for her. That's how it was when I met Jason in the Keys. Take some time for you. It might be a bit scary at first but it will be the best Christmas gift you give yourself. A bit of TLC." Maddy sat still by Greg as she watched her ex-husband continue to stare off into the distance.

"I must have sounded like a fool at the hospital," Greg said shaking his head. "I had this idea that you'd leave your husband and come running back to me if I made all these changes. Like the ones we talked about when we were married but I was too stubborn to listen back then. I knew you were married and Hope told me how happy you were. I'm sorry if this ruined your Christmas. I guess I figured if I couldn't be happy, no one else was supposed to be either."

"That's just it. You can be happy if you choose to. Will it look like what you expected? Probably not but it's your choice Greg. Your choice."

"Thanks, Maddy and I'm really sorry. My mom always said you were a smart one. And sweet. She was right on both accounts." Greg finally looked at her. She hoped that she had helped and not hurt him because she wanted the pain of the past to be gone for both of them. Not just for their sakes but for their daughter and granddaughter too.

"I always did like your Momma," Maddy said with a smile.

"I know this is going to sound weird but can I give you a hug?" Greg asked. "As a thank you for putting up with all this nonsense?"

Then Maddy did something she never thought she would ever do again once they had left the courtroom the day of their divorce: she gave Greg a sincere hug.

"You're going to be fine but all this between you and me is settled, right? I think Jason has reached his limit on this little situation. We were about to talk to the police to secure a restraining order but didn't want to upset Hope!" Maddy said.

"Ah, looking back now, I can see where your husband might want to do that. Again, I feel like a fool. Things just feel lonely."

"You have a daughter that loves you, your parents and friends. But take some advice from me if you want: for once, like I said before, find you and then that special someone is going to come into your life. And when that happens, you're going to be amazed. I'm speaking from experience: it's wonderful." Maddy backed away and could see Greg's face completely changed from when they had walked out onto the porch. He looked like he had lost a battle but was going to be okay.

"Now, I'm ready to concentrate on our little granddaughter. She is going to need some happy and fun grandparents, right?"

"Most definitely. And Maddy?"

"Yes, Greg?"

"Thank you. And Merry Christmas."

"Merry Christmas Greg."

13

When they walked back into the house, Jason immediately looked at Maddy for some confirmation that everything was okay. She smiled at her husband and blew him a kiss.

"Where did you two wander off to?" Hope asked.

"I needed to talk to your Dad for a minute," Maddy said.

"Everything okay?"

"We're just excited about this new baby girl in our lives. Can't wait to spoil her rotten," Greg said, sitting beside his daughter.

"Everything okay?" Jason whispered in Maddy's ear.

"I hope so. I'll tell you more on the way home."

"I still can't believe he was that desperate," Jason said, looking at the sand during their walk along the beach as the sun was setting. Christmas lights were beginning to illuminate most of beach houses as they passed by.

"He's really lost right now. That's how he described it. I kinda know how he feels."

"You do?" Jason asked puzzled.

"I mean I did. When I got divorced, it was a crazy time but I did just the opposite of Greg. Whereas he was dating and got married and divorced twice, I avoided everyone except family and close friends. Everyone encouraged me to date but all I could see is being hurt all over again. But then I met you." Maddy curled up to Jason's side, putting her arm around his waist. "You changed everything for me when we met in the Florida Keys."

"Glad I could help," Jason teased. "I hope he really leaves you alone now. I guess only time will tell."

"True. It'll be interesting for sure with the grandbaby coming. But I think we'll be able to work things out. I hope he finds someone as special to him as you are to me."

Jason slowed to a stop and pulled Maddy closer into his arms. The wind was a bit chilly but there was an inviting warmth that spread between him and his wife. With the last bit of sun setting, it gave Maddy a soft glow and she looked so beautiful.

"Why are you staring at me like that?" Maddy asked.

"I'm so incredibly lucky."

"I think we both are." With the sounds of the ocean waves coming to shore and Christmas lights twinkling in the distance, Jason kissed Maddy with so much passion that it left her weak in the knees.

"You know I have one more present for you at home," Maddy said teasingly.

"You do?" Jason asked perplexed but then saw the look in his wife's eyes.

"I think you might really like it or should I say enjoy this one. And I saved it especially for this evening."

"Then why are we walking the beach?" Jason said, still holding her tight.

"Merry Christmas, Jason."

"Merry Christmas, Maddy."

"They're here!" Maddy cried out with delight. She hurried down the front steps, forgetting the coat by the door.

"Wow, when you said beach house, I didn't know it was like this," Riley said. "This makes your house in the Keys look like a playroom."

"I'm so glad you're here!" Maddy and Riley hugged, giggling the whole time. "A whole week together!"

"Yes, and I can't wait."

As soon as the luggage was inside and everyone was settled into their rooms until the New Year's Eve festivities, Riley snuck into Maddy's bedroom and the two of them lay across the king size bed like they used to in high school.

"Wow, this has been a year," Riley said looking over to Maddy.

"I know it's been a wild ride for me. The Florida Keys by myself. Meeting Jason. Dealing with Andrea!"

"How could I forgot about that slut," Riley said which made Maddy laugh.

"Yeah, I think she might even be worse than my ex," Maddy said, "and that's a tough one."

"Then you got married, moved here, going to be a grandma and now you have a house in Florida too. And I thought my life was exciting," Riley laughed.

"Well, you've been with me through most of it."

"Very true."

Both women relaxed in silence thinking about the past year.

"You know, Riley, I never imagined that I would find anyone else. I was actually content to grow old by myself. Maybe get a dog."

"Yeah, right. You think I'd let you do that?" Riley snickered.

Maddy laughed. "No, you'd have definitely lined up one blind date after another. Remember some of the dates you fixed up for me in college? That was the worse!"

"Hey, some weren't so bad. How about Michael? He was pretty cute!"

"And flirted with every girl including some of the professors," Maddy chided.

"True but damn was he good looking."

They both were silent remembering their past. They had been friends for so long, helping each other through the good and the bad. Maddy only wished they lived closer but the house Jason had purchased in the Keys would mean the two friends would be together more often.

"So, what's on tap tonight?" Riley asked.

"It's up to you guys," Maddy said. "You're the ones that just drove twelve hours straight. Didn't know if you wanted to ring in the New Year here or go to the Flip Flop Drop." Maddy couldn't help but laugh at the look on her friend's face.

"What the hell is a Flip Flop Drop?"

"You know how they have the ball drop on Times Square to ring in the New Year? Well, here on Folly Beach, we do the same thing except it's a giant pair of flip-flops that drop till the clock strikes midnight and brings in the New Year. It's on Center Street, an easy walk from here. There are all kinds of things going on: music, dancing, food."

"I vote for a nap then we go join the festivities. I know Carter and the kids would love it too!" Riley said. "Are you feeling up to it?"

"Yes! I was hoping you'd want to go but driving that long – I wasn't sure. Then tomorrow we have something special for New Year's Day."

"What?"

"Can't tell you till tomorrow. It's a secret," Maddy said.

"Now this really reminds me of our college days!" Riley laughed. "Let me go tell Carter about tonight and I'm going to lay down for a bit. I'd rather stay here and talk but we have all week. At this point I might even let Carter go back by himself and stay here longer. All I need is my laptop to work."

"You can stay as long as you want Riley. I'm just glad you're here," Maddy said, hugging her best friend before Riley left the room.

14

"Are you sure you want to do this? I've done it twice and my body let me know that I had lost my marbles. I was hurting so bad afterwards but I thought it was just from the cold. Now I know it was from the cold and this illness. But if my doctors would let me and I knew I wouldn't have any problems, I'd be going in with you guys," Maddy said as she, Jason, Riley and Carter stood on the beach with hundreds of other people near the Folly Beach pier. It was the annual Polar Bear Plunge and with the unusually cold weather, the ocean temperature was a nice fifty-two degrees.

"I don't want to sound like a controlling husband but there is no way you're doing this. Except for your feet and I'm still wondering if that is a good idea," Jason said giving her a wink.

"Well as soon as you come out of the water, I have towels for everyone and a few blankets. I have a feeling you are going to need it. Then I will walk in the surf like I do each year. How long I walk will depend on how my feet hold up in the cold water."

"This is awesome," Riley said, wearing a pair of pajama pants and a long sleeve shirt.

"I can't believe I'm doing this," Carter said, standing by Riley. "Wait till I tell the guys at work."

"I feel the same way but then it's something new to try," Jason said and both men bumped fists.

"But after this I want to go back and chill for the day. We stayed up late last night watching all the antics around here though it was fun watching the excitement. And I thought Riley would never go to bed when we got back," Jason said only to look at Riley who was sticking her tongue out at him. "Remember – this isn't that nice warm water of the Florida Keys."

"We can handle it," Riley said. "Right Carter?"

"I'm not sure but I think we're about to find out."

"I'm going to watch from over here and hope to get some pictures," Maddy told them. "Good luck!"

Everyone was lining up behind the starting line marked by yellow tape. It was only a matter of minutes before the swarm of people would be dashing into the ocean as part of a tradition for many that lived by the beach.

Maddy heard the countdown and she stood back, ready to video her husband's plunge into the frigid ocean water. There were so many people but that only made the activity more festive and a fun way to start the New Year.

Suddenly they were off. Maddy was able to keep the camera on Jason as he ran into the water, ducked beneath a wave and then ran like a mad man back toward the beach. She quickly spotted Riley and Carter who were moving just as fast.

"Damn, that was cold!" he said hopping up and down trying to get warm.

"I can't feel my legs," Riley cried, "but that was so cool!"

"I'll never complain about the water temperature in Florida again!" Carter said, wrapping a towel and blanket around him to try to get dry and warm at the same time.

"Hold still, silly, and I'll put the blanket around you," Maddy said doing her best not to laugh at her husband. "I told you it was a bit painful."

"My legs feel like needles are sticking me everywhere. And people do this up north in the ice? No way I would try that! This was plenty cold for me."

"Are you warming up at all?" Maddy asked as the trio stood there, wrapped up but still shivering.

"Maybe just a little," Jason said. "Are you going in the surf now? I know you like the feel of the ocean on your feet but that is a bit too cold."

"I won't stay long, I promise. I'll get a picture of my feet in the water then leave. But I've done this every year, even in the rain. I'll be right back."

Maddy walked toward the surf as most people were running back out of the water. She dodged people here and there but finally found a small spot where she walked quickly in the water, got a picture of her feet in the ocean surf then was swiftly by her husband's side. It was cold today but she was bundled up good and Maddy loved the ocean. The sound of the waves, the sand beneath her feet, the cold ocean water, shore birds skittering about – all of it fed her soul. But as she looked back to Jason, he was the one that had truly helped her heal and feel happy again.

"Hard to walk now isn't it?" Jason asked as she reached him, quickly grabbing a towel to wrap her feet.

"Wow! That was a bit cold! I can only imagine how you guys feel. At least I'm getting feeling back in my feet. How are ya'll doing?" she said, still chuckling at her handsome husband with his wet head, unshaven face and beautiful eyes.

"I'm fine now that you're here," and he pulled her into the blanket with him.

"Now I'm all wet," Maddy said. But she didn't care. With all the clothes she had on, she was sure the water wouldn't touch her skin. And anyway, they were really close to home. Instead, she loved being next to her husband, bundled up close with the ocean as their background.

"Hey you two, remember you're in public," Riley scolded with a smile.

"This has been a heck of a holiday," Jason said, resting his head on top of hers. "But it's been wonderful. I'm so blessed to have shared it with you. I love you Maddy, more than I can say."

"And I love you. But you get to plan the next holiday."

"At least that gives me some time to keep us really busy," Jason replied, putting on some dry clothes over the wet ones till they could reach their house.

"Not Christmas, but Valentine's Day. That's next month you know," Maddy said giving him a sly glance.

"Oh, I can come up with some very interesting ideas for that holiday. You just wait and see," Jason said with his eyebrows raised.

"I'm definitely looking forward to it." Maddy replied with a smile.

"Happy New Year, Maddy."

"Happy New Year, my love."

Author's Note:

I hope you have enjoyed this story of Jason and Maddy's first Christmas. To find out how their relationship began when Maddy's was visiting the Florida Keys, you can read "The Keys to Love". I hope you enjoy it!

Acknowledgements

First and foremost, I have to thank all my readers! You are the best and I feel so blessed that you have embraced me as an author and a woman who loves to share my passions for all things creative on my website and social media platforms. Your support means the world to me.

A shout out to my fellow indie authors who are making strides in this wild, wonderful world of writing and publishing books. As all of us work together, we are sharing our stories and gifts with the world, which is so important.

Endless thanks to my husband, Jeff, who continues to support me on this journey. He takes over when I'm in "writer's mode" which is a blessing because if he didn't, we wouldn't have a clean dish to eat on or freshly washed clothes to wear! You are my rock and I love you.

Also, a special thanks to my awesome, wonderful, terrific – I could go on and on – parents, Sonny and Irene. Dad, you help me so much as I navigate the business side of being an author and creative person. Mom, your patience as my sounding board is unbelievable – you deserve more than the words written on this page. I love you both!

Other Novels
By Miki Bennett

"The Florida Keys Novels" series:

The Keys to Love

Forever in the Keys

Run Away to the Keys

Back to the Keys

A Wedding in the Keys

From the Keys to Montana – A Novella

"Camping in High Heels" series:

Camping in High Heels

Camping in High Heels: Las Vegas

Camping in High Heels: California

Camping in High Heels: Yellowstone

"The Nauterian Novels":

"She Came from the Sea" novella

About the Author

Miki Bennett is the best-selling author of three novel series: *The Florida Keys Novels, Camping in High Heels* series, and *The Nauterian Novels*. She has won numerous awards for both her novels and art.

When she's not writing, Miki enjoys going to the beach, spending time outdoors, trying new art techniques or figuring out the newest tech gadget. She lives in Charleston, South Carolina, with her husband, Jeff, and little dog, Emma.

You can connect with Miki at her website: www.mikibennett. com and on Facebook, Instagram and Pinterest.